BABY FOR THE OFF LIMITS SINGLE DADDY

CALLIE STEVENS

1

JUNE

I'm not sure how long I've been walking. I don't even know where I'm going. All I know is I have to get as far away from that house as possible. But walking in the depths of Chicago winter and pulling a rolling suitcase is not a recipe for success.

I'm shivering. I didn't even get to grab my hat. My ears feel like they could fall off. I should just call a car. Or someone... but I'm in fucking shock. I can't bring myself to pull my phone out of my pocket and call an Uber.

I've never been fired before. I love my job. And, I have to say, I'm pretty damn good at it. I've been nannying ever since I graduated high school. That's eight years, not to mention all the babysitting I did in my teen years. What's that saying? Do the thing you love and you won't work a day in your life? Well, that's me and working with kids. For every annoyance, I can think of five things I love about the job.

This is the first family that I've had a problem with. Or should I say, had a problem with me... I'm really not sure yet.

Fuck, the kids. Harvey and Ellen. They were perfect in nearly every way. I've never left a family I've nannied for without saying goodbye to the kids. None of this is *their* fault. Why should they have to be punished?

Saying this is unprecedented would be an understatement.

Don't look back, Juniper. Just keep walking.

It's hard not to believe I did anything wrong. But I know I didn't. Shame is burning at the corners of my eyes, although it might just be the cold. Her words echo in my brain over and over: "Get the fuck out before I ruin your life."

And they owe me for last week. Doubt that'll ever come now.

I finally get to a Starbucks and force myself inside, suitcase and all. I don't care how haggard or ridiculous I look. I pull out my phone; I'd love to call my mom and dad. I just want to hear their voices. But now that they're in Florida, they're hard to get in touch with. They're always doing something. Bingo. Canasta. Tanning. The number of messages I've left them asking them to call me is staggering. Shouldn't it be the other way around? Shouldn't *they* be begging to hear from *me*? I'm the girl trying to live it up in her mid-twenties! Except all I seem to be doing is worrying and panicking all the time. I thought I had it all under control.

I can't even go home. I was living with the family full-time. So, naturally, I rented out my house in Mayfair for the year. Get a little extra income. There's still two weeks left on the lease.

I literally have nowhere to go. Nowhere! That's... well, that's not something I ever thought I'd say. My parents don't seem to want to hear from me, all my friends have their shit on lock, whether it's their corporate job or getting married. Next thing I know, everyone's going to be having kids and I'll still be sitting in a Starbucks wondering what the hell to do with my life.

I know there is one person I can call. Keifer. My best friend in the whole world. He'll always pick up. But I don't want to be a burden to him.

I pull up the Uber app, but I don't know where it could possibly take me. I could stay at a hotel, but two weeks at a hotel would be detrimental to my bank account.

At that very moment, my phone vibrates. An Instagram notification. From the man himself.

He's just sent me a meme, nothing important. We're always sending things back and forth to each other. Doesn't matter, the content of the message isn't what's important.

It's the reminder that he's there. Available if I let myself ask. That's my person.

Keifer will always help me. I pick up the suitcase and leave the café.

———

As soon as the elevator doors open and I see Keifer standing there, I run into his arms.

"Yo, what the hell is going on?"

All the emotions that have been frozen inside me, literally and figuratively, burble up onto the surface. I start to weep onto the lapel of his suit jacket.

"Oh my god, June..."

Keifer is the only thing I have left of my childhood. My best friend since kindergarten. The only person I can trust. Feeling his arms wrapped around me brings me back to reality.

"What happened?" he asks, pulling away to look at my face. His light green eyes plead with me to let him in on the secret.

"I need help, Keifer."

Keifer looks nervously around the reception area. "Let's go to my office." He fights me for my suitcase, waving my hand off the handle. It brings a small smile to my face. We make our way through the halls of Hawthorn, Inc. Thankfully, we don't run into his dad or either of his brothers. That would just be embarrassing, even though I'm practically a member of the Hawthorn family at this point. They've taken me in as one of their own, even more so since my parents moved away.

But right now, I'd be mortified to see them.

"Sit down. You want a coffee?"

I nod and grab a tissue to wipe my nose as I sit down in the chair across from his desk. It's always a funny feeling that we're the same age and he's the Chief Operating Officer for a Fortune 500 company and I play hide and seek for a living.

"Okay," Keifer says, bringing me a cup from his personal pot. Keifer always has the best coffee and orders it from all over. "What happened?"

"I got fired."

He raises his eyebrows. "I know. You told me that much on the phone. But what happened?"

I screw my lips together tightly. "I don't want to talk about it. It just happened and it all happened so fast and now I have nowhere to go and–"

"Hey, hey, hey, slow down. You're talking a mile a minute."

I look up at him sheepishly. It's too embarrassing. I'd rather forget all about it than relive it.

"You can tell me, June..."

I shake my head and look away. "I know. I just... I really can't handle talking about it yet. Please understand." He nods.

"And I don't know where I'm gonna go. The renters are still at my house until the end of the month and–"

"Stay with me!" Keifer says enthusiastically.

Despite my emotional state, I can't help bursting into laughter. "No fucking way."

"Why not? You'd have your own room, it'd–"

"I'm not staying in 'the man cave'," I say, deepening my voice. That's my affectionate name for Keifer's bachelor pad. It's definitely clear a single guy lives there. It's messy, it's poorly decorated, and he's frequently out of toilet paper. "I may be desperate, but I have standards."

Keifer chuckles, "Okay. Fair. You could stay up in Wilmette. My dad has plenty of space."

"No, him and Rye need all the space they can get," I say. "What with the baby due in two months."

He leans on the edge of his desk and crosses his arms, raising his gaze into the air, calculating, thinking. "Do you have any plans that are going to keep you in the city for the next two months?"

I snort. "Me? Plans? No." Nannying for *that* family took up nearly all of my free time.

"Then why don't you stay at the cabin?"

I raise an eyebrow. "By myself?"

Keifer shrugs. "Why not?"

"Because the cabin's not like a cute little place, it's like a fucking mansion, Keif."

"So what? How much mess can you make? There's only one of you. Besides, I'll send in the housekeeper afterward," he says as if it's no big thing.

Keifer and I met when his family was still normal. Or normal enough. When his dad's company blew up, their quality of life did too. Mine stayed the same, although I spent a lot of time knocking elbows with the Hawthorns, which meant joining them on family trips, for big parties, and, of course, weekends at the "cabin" in Michigan. "I don't know. That's a lot of space for just one person."

"I'll have the fridge stocked when you get there. You can even borrow one of the cars," he says.

"No, I can't borrow a car either, I–"

"*Juniper.*"

I seal my mouth shut. I know he's serious when he uses my full name.

"Let me help you."

I sigh. "It's too much, though, Keif, it's–"

"You're my best friend. My sister even if not by blood. I'd do anything for you," he says, eyes steeled in mine.

I know he would. Keifer would give me an organ. I would do the same for him. This commitment to each other is why people have been suspicious our whole lives that we're something more than friends. But we both know that our soul connection is not romantic. Don't get me wrong, Keifer's handsome. The second tallest of his brothers, with the signature sharp Hawthorn jaw line, and a mop of blond hair that makes him look like the cute boy next door from a nineties sitcom. Some might think I'm crazy not to try and hop on that. But I couldn't. He's Keifer. I remember when he ate an entire ChapStick in the first grade.

"Okay," I say softly, tears bubbling into my eyes again. "You have no idea how much this means to me."

"Of course, I do," he says. Then, he goes to the door. "Now, what kind of car do you want? Maserati? Jaguar?"

I laugh and get to my feet. "Maybe not something so... expensive. Something practical."

"June, now is not a time for practicality," he says, holding out his arm for me.

I take it and smile at him. "Well, it at least needs to be good in the snow."

"I've got the perfect thing," he says with a chipper smile. "Now, come along. To the garage!"

2

JARRED

Finance is nothing like it seems in the movies. There's a lot of spreadsheets, coffee, and lots of meetings that could have been emails.

Don't get me wrong, I'm lucky. I know I'm lucky. I mean, aside from being top of my graduating class at University of Chicago and aside from being in Crain's "40 Under 40" when I was twenty-three. I'm lucky. Not everyone's dad runs a multi-billion-dollar corporation. I still work my ass off, but nepotism isn't so bad now and again. Not to mention working with my brothers makes it a whole family affair, which is good. And, most importantly, I like what I do. I like crunching numbers and spreadsheets. They're something you can count on. Two plus two will always be four and the quadratic equation will never add any new letters.

Math will always be there when life goes topsy turvy.

Today, though, it is not good. Oliver, the middle child in every way including attitude, has imposed a new cyber security measure without clearing it with me. Consequently, our numbers are all fucking wrong. Security is never a bad investment these days, but can't the guy tell me the numbers?

On top of that, Keifer's gone MIA. So, the Chief Security Officer's fucked me over and the Chief Operating Officer is nowhere to be found for me to complain to?

I need a break or I'll just punch someone in the face .

The blare of my cell phone makes my brain grind to a halt. A call from Miss Rebecca. Shit. I answer without hesitation. "Hello?"

"Mr. Hawthorn?"

I cringe at the moniker. I'm not quite thirty yet but being called "Mr. Hawthorn" makes me feel ancient. "Miss Rebecca! Is everything alright?"

The pre-school teacher sighs heavily and I'm already bracing myself against the desk. "I'm afraid Piper's having another hard day."

"Oh god," I mutter and pinch my nose bridge. *Another one.* The third one since they've returned from Christmas break. I knew preschool would be hard on her, but I thought it was time to get out there and make friends, not be stuck at home with a nanny. And she took to it like a fish to water. She always came home with so many crafts and stories about new friends.

But since Christmas, she's been having outbursts to the point of inconsolable tears.

"I'm sorry, Miss Rebecca, this is–"

"It's okay," Miss Rebecca replies in her sweetest preschool teacher voice. Her patience seems limitless. "It's a normal phase. I'm just concerned that we haven't figured out how best to help her yet."

I sigh, "Trust me, she adores you guys. It's not to do with you."

"Oh, I know. I've been around the block before. I can

tell when a kid actually hates me," she says through a wry laugh, one I cannot reciprocate right now.

I glance out the window. It's a desperate, gray Chicago day. The clouds are heavy with snow. We're supposed to get a huge blizzard tonight. "What happened this time?" I ask softly.

"Well, we were celebrating a birthday. A student had her mom and dad come in. And Piper was fine through the celebration. It wasn't until the parents actually left that we noticed something was wrong."

My heart shatters. "Is this normal? To be so upset when–"

"Piper's perceiving the world around her more clearly. You know, she's in a phase of noticing similarities and differences. And this difference is hard to cope with."

"I've been reading her all those books you recommended, I–"

"It'll sink in. It might just take some time. Some more conversations maybe."

Maybe *I* need to read some more books too. On being a single parent. Most of the literature out there is for single moms. The stuff out there for single dads is often focused on divorce and being widowered. Where's the literature for a guy whose ex wants nothing to do with her child?

I get up and go to the closet in my office to grab my coat. "I'll come get her right away."

"That would probably be best," she replies. "Drive safe."

This day could not be going worse. This week, this month. I'd say year, but it's only just started. Although if this is an omen of things to come, I should quit while I'm ahead. As I shrug my coat on, the door to my office bursts open.

"What's with this reversal?" Oliver asks loudly.

"Oliver, I can't talk right now, I have to go," I say and try to brush past him, but it's hard when he fills up the whole doorway in all directions.

"You can't reverse a decision in *my* department."

I huff, "Yes, I can when you don't have the proper budget clearance to move forward with it. Two-hundred grand isn't just fun money, Oliver."

"No, I think you just want to boss me around."

Not this. Not this brotherly rivalry thing. Not today. "Dude, I don't have time for this."

Oliver pushes my shoulders like when we were kids and something's about to go down. I trip backward, my shaggy hair flopping around my face. "You too scared to face me?"

"You want your fucking clearance? Fine. Go wild. Spend the entire budget. See if I give a fuck," I spit. Then, I shove him out of the way and leave my office, running smack into my dad.

"What's going on?" he asks with a frown. "We're not still on the budget issue, are we?"

"He reversed the purchase. I look like a fucking fool now," Oliver shouts.

"Lower your voice," Dad says soothingly. "Jarred, why are you dressed to go? Where are you going?"

I look between the two of them and swallow. "I have to go pick up Piper. She's having another bad day."

Oliver's anger immediately fades. "Well, you didn't say that."

"You didn't give me a chance!"

"I wouldn't have been mad if I had known–"

"Boys. Cut it out," Dad says in a stern voice. "Oliver, go back to your department."

Oliver and I exchange an awkward look. There's only a

year between us; we can be the best of friends or worst of enemies. But one thing is certain. Whenever Piper is involved, our beef goes away. He starts to go past us, back to the security wing, muttering, "Sorry, man," in my ear as he goes.

Dad touches my back lightly. "Let me walk you to the elevator."

I explain to him the situation as we go. Dad is pretty good when it comes to parenting advice. He was remarkably good at it for becoming a father at such a young age. Maybe that's why he's so excited to be having a baby on the way now that he's forty-six. Get to work all those muscles again. "I'm just not sure what more I can do," I say with a heavy sigh. "Apart from somehow getting back together with Meredith or–"

"No, definitely not," Dad says, visibly wincing at the mention of her name.

I'd never want to. After all, we're divorced. But if it would fix what's happening with Piper, I'd do just about anything.

"I'm sorry."

I frown. "For what?"

"I can't imagine the baby is helping anything," he says as off-handedly as he can.

"No, Dad, Piper's so excited to meet the baby, you know that."

He nods. "I know, but she knows she's not going to be the baby of the family much longer and maybe she knows I'm not going to be able to give her the same amount of attention as–"

"Stop," I cut him off. "That's... I don't think that's what's going on."

From the corner of my eye, I see him relax the slightest bit.

"I'm so tired, Dad," I say.

"I know you are," he says. "I can tell. Just from the way you walk."

I press the button for the elevator and tap my foot as I wait. "I think I might need some time off."

"I think that'd be a good idea."

I give him a terrified look. I didn't think he'd actually agree. "Seriously?"

"Seriously," he says with a soft nod. "You and Piper need to get away and just be together for a bit. She needs her time with you."

I smile sadly. "You're probably right."

"Why don't you go to the cabin? Get out of town. Turn on your out-of-office reply. I'll cover for you," Dad says with a sneaky smile.

I raise my eyebrows. "Are you encouraging me to play hooky?"

Dad shrugs and smiles. "Maybe."

I laugh. Ever since Dad got into his new relationship, he's been a lot more light-hearted. Footloose and fancy-free, as the saying goes. I'm happy for him. He deserves it. Even if his fiancée is the same age as me. Who cares, if they're happy?

The elevator arrives. Game time decision. "Are you *sure*?" I ask cautiously.

"Totally."

"But really sure?"

"Really, really sure. Take a week. Take two! We'll be okay. In fact, you and Oliver could use some space from each other," he jokes.

I step into the elevator. Before the door can close, I throw my hand out. "Are you *sure* sure?"

"Jare, I'm sure," he murmurs. "Get the hell out of here."

I smile.

"And tell Piper that Grampa misses her," he says with an excitable smile.

"I will, Dad." I press the button for the parking garage and take a deep breath. "Thanks."

Dad doesn't respond, just gives me a sly smile. Our secret. That's the privilege of our relationship with me as his first child. Even though I wasn't the only one for long, we've always maintained a special bond. He knows how much pressure got put on me when we were kids to set a good example, especially once Mom died. Now, he does his best to be my partner in crime.

And I'm not going to lie. It's gonna be nice to get the fuck out of here.

———

When I arrive at Piper's preschool, she's sitting in the front office with one of the teacher's aides. She's settled down at least enough to enjoy singing nursery rhymes with her teacher. But as soon as she sees me, she leaps up and throws herself into my arms. "Daddy! I thought I'd never see you again!"

I can't help but chuckle, leaning my face into her hair. Dark blonde like me and Keifer, my baby brother. I hold her in my arms as tight as can be. "Now that's just silly. Where would I go without you, Pipes?"

She giggles into my chest, arms encircled around my neck.

The teacher's aide, a quirky little brunette with big

glasses, hands me her backpack. "Thank you," I say with a solemn smile.

"You're welcome," she says. "Bye, Piper. I hope you feel better."

"Thank you," Piper says without drawing her head up.

The aide pouts her lips softly, so endeared by my daughter.

"Um, hey, Piper's going to be out of school for a few days. Who should I let know about that?" I say to her.

"You can send an email to Miss Rebecca and CC the front desk."

I thank her and start to head out of the school to the car.

"Where are we going, Daddy?" Piper asks, raising her head to look at me.

I smile at her, hiking her up further on my hip. "We're going on an adventure, Piper. Just you and me. "

Her tear-stained face lightens and a big grin spreads onto her face.

3

———

JUNE

Keifer was right. This is exactly what I needed.

After Keifer walked me to the Bentley, I immediately threw my suitcase in the back and made the two-and-a-half-hour drive to Glenn, Michigan, where the Hawthorn cabin is. Situated at the end of a sweeping private drive, shrouded in pines and leafless trees, the cabin welcomed me, cast in a warm light that illuminated the darkness.

Every time I'm here, I laugh to myself that they call it a cabin. It's a gigantic compound with literal *wings*. The only thing rustic about it is that it's made of wood.

It even has a name emblazoned on a little wooden sign: The Hawthorn Haven. Now if that's not a rich people thing, I don't know what is.

When I arrived, I went immediately into the kitchen and checked the pantry which was, as Keifer promised, stocked with food. All of my favorites which Keifer knows well from all the years we've been friends. I immediately gorged on a whole bag of Goldfish. I hadn't eaten anything all day. Then, I plopped in front of the mammoth flatscreen in the family room with the humongous, vaulted ceilings and fell promptly asleep. I needed it.

This morning, after waking up crunchily on the couch with Goldfish crumbs on my chest, I made myself at home, more like a guest than a runaway. I chose the room I've always had, in the west wing at the end of the hallway, across from the mounted deer head that I've never had the courage to ask if it's real or not.

Even though I'm the only one here, this room makes me feel safe and protected. There *are* people who care for me. Well, at least one.

I'm no stranger to being alone. In fact, I'm so used to it that it's the default. It's only moments like this that I realize how much it'd be nice to share my life with someone, anyone. Someone whose presence doesn't feel conditional.

After freshening up and showering, I did a final check of everything in the house to make sure I had everything I needed in case the incoming snowstorm proved blizzard worthy. No surprise, the place is stocked stem to stern with anything you could possibly need. Not just the food, but toiletries, entertainment, *everything*. Hell, there's even a home gym!

In the afternoon, I took a walk around the grounds. There's a fantastic view of the lake, a desperate amount of feet below the edge of the property. Lake Michigan is still beautiful in the winter even though it's gray and rather desolate.

And then, I decided to make myself a nice dinner. The kitchen is state of the art and while I'm no Michelin star chef, I can whip up something nice for myself. Mashed potatoes, asparagus, a lovely piece of salmon. I'm treating myself like a queen, even though I'm just tiptoeing around with my hair in a messy bun on my head, clad in a big T-shirt and shorts.

The house is toasty, with heated floors and warmth emanating from the walls. It's as if it's not even winter out. However, I can hear the wind whipping against the windows every so often.

There's a storm coming.

I decide to eat dinner in front of the television and watch a comfort movie. Something that will make me cry. I think those things are synonymous.

Just as I'm scrolling through options on Hulu (after trolling Netflix and not being able to find anything), remote in one hand, forkful of mashed potatoes in the other, a head-light passes through the huge living room windows. I get to my feet and cautiously walk up to the window, peeking out into the dark night. Luckily, the lights over the driveway let me see that it's a luxury car, its smooth lines glistening.

I smile to myself. It must be Keifer come to surprise me, to take a long weekend and just veg with me. He's the *best*.

And just in time too. Snow is starting to fall from the sky. It's light now, but midwestern snowstorms are lethal for how unassuming they seem at first.

I'm sure he's got a lot of luggage (the Hawthorn boys always do), so I run to the door to meet him.

This is going to be the best weekend ever.

4

———

JARRED

I wring my hands around the steering wheel and stare at Hawthorn Haven. It's lit up like a Christmas tree, which is desperately unsettling. The house seems to be alive with activity, as if all of us Hawthorns were staying there, and I just ran out to pick up a bottle of whisky.

Who is here? My brothers aren't. Dad and Rye aren't. I don't think we offered it to any clients for the weekend.

I glance back at Piper. She's passed out in her car seat, her little mouth lolling open. Thank God.

I leave the car running and step out cautiously. The wind whips around me, snowflakes dancing. The storm's about to settle in. There's no turning back to Chicago, that's for damn sure. The clouds followed us all the way here, a looming threat.

I start toward the door and then stop. What if I'm walking into a dangerous situation? Squatters? Robbers? I need a weapon. I circle the car and open the trunk. There's not much to work with. Mostly just odds and ends from Piper I've thrown back here over the past few months. A macaroni art that never made it into the house, a stuffed giraffe, a smushed up coloring book. Shit. I'm without a paddle.

I root around for a minute when my hand lands on a cool piece of metal. I yank on it and pull a tire iron out of the trunk. This will do. If I'm convicted of second-degree murder, it will be in self-defense.

I turn back to the front door, hiding the tire iron in the pleats of my coat. The wind is picking up, even in the minute I've been out here. I stalk toward the door carefully, my heart beating heavily. I'm not a violent person. The most I've ever done in my life is roughhoused with my brothers. But if it comes down to it, I'll do anything to protect Piper.

Suddenly, the door to the cabin flies open. I reflexively lift the tire iron and shout, "Don't move or I'll–" I stop when I recognize who it is.

There, in the doorway of the cabin, is Juniper Reed, Keifer's best friend. Honorary member of the Hawthorn clan. I'm struck by how the light from the house filters out around her, highlighting her long, lithe legs that extend effortlessly from the tiny shorts she's wearing.

"June?!" I cry out in shock.

"Jarred?!" she echoes with just as much surprise. "What are you doing here?"

I drop my arm, trying to hide the tire iron from sight. "What are *you* doing here?"

June blinks. "I'm staying here."

"Well, *I'm* staying here."

We're trapped in a loop of confusion. The storm is getting worse by the second. This is a stupid conversation to have in the freezing cold. "Let's have this conversation inside, huh?"

"Is Piper with you?" June asks, gesturing to the car that's still running.

Piper. Of course. "Um, yeah."

"Here, I'll get her and you can get your bags and things," June offers.

June's always been really good with Piper. After all, she works with kids for a living. And Piper's always been fond of her. I have so many questions, but for now, we have to get out of this storm. "Okay, sounds good."

June disappears into the house briefly and reemerges wearing a coat and some moccasins. Her naked legs peek out from below the coat, and I can't help but keep glancing at them. She hurries toward the car to fetch Piper. I shake off my distractedness and follow her.

I can't help but watch as June gently jostles Piper's leg and coos, "Piper... wake up..."

Piper's eyes blear open and adjust to the face in front of her. "Hm? Are we here?"

"Yes, honey. Now come on."

Piper doesn't even seem to wonder why it's June and not me waking her up. I guess she's just been that integrated into her life. Into all of our lives. She's been Keifer's best friend since they were practically in diapers. She's an honorary Hawthorn and Piper's never known any different. I'm grateful for that.

I retrieve the bags while June carries Piper inside. When I finally step inside, out of the cold and into the warmth of the cabin, I can breathe a sigh of relief.

"What are you doing here, June?" Piper asks with her arms spread wide as June unzips her coat off her.

"Well, Uncle Keifer suggested I stay here for a couple weeks because there are people staying at my house," June says in a sweet voice.

I frown. Doesn't June live with the family she works

for? In the Gold Cost, or something. I decide to save that question for later.

"But *we're* staying here," Piper replies giddily.

"I know, it seems that some wires were crossed," June says with a shrug. "But of all the people to show up late at night, I'm glad it's you." She pokes Piper in the belly and my little girl squeals with laughter.

I haven't even taken off my coat. I'm still so confused at what's going on.

"Smells good!" Piper announces.

"Oh, you got here just in time, I just made dinner! How about you go pick out a movie and I'll make you a plate, hm?"

Piper stomps her feet excitedly and rushes off into the family room without another thought.

Left alone, June and I look at each other awkwardly. "You want to go talk in the kitchen?" she asks, pointing down the hall.

"Sounds good," I say, more curtly than I mean too.

June is a friend, certainly. She joins us for our Sunday dinners almost every week. But we're more polite to each other than friendly. We've rarely ever had one on one conversations, even as kids. I've always just been old enough to have a life separate from Keifer. And I spent, well, all of my twenties steeped in the disastrous romance with my ex-wife. June has always just kind of been set dressing in the movie of my life. Pretty, sweet set dressing. But still.

When we make it to the kitchen, I am greeted with the scents of a delicious, savory meal. I can't keep from salivating.

"So, you guys are staying here for the weekend?" June asks as she starts to fix a plate for Piper.

I watch her spoon potatoes onto a plate. "Um, yeah. Maybe a little longer."

"Oh. Okay," June says, her eyes flicking nervously to mine. June's got the strangest eyes I've ever seen. One of them is hazel, green intermingling with golden brown like a forest at daybreak. The other, the deepest darkest brown you can imagine. They're fascinating. I've always wanted to ask why her eyes are like that, but I've never had the courage. "Well..." she glances out the window. "I don't feel comfortable driving in this storm right now, but–"

"Of course, I wouldn't ask you to leave, especially not tonight. And if you need somewhere to stay..." I trail off, an implicit question in my words.

June sighs. "I lost my job. Yesterday."

"Oh, God. June, I'm sorry."

She shakes her head. "It's for the best. I just needed somewhere to go and asked Keifer for help. He suggested I come here and now I'm here and now you're here and there's a snowstorm and–"

I chuckle which stops her rambling. "My dad suggested Piper and I come here to get away. So, it sounds like everyone had the same idea."

She smiles half-heartedly. "Seems like it."

"I hope we're not ruining your plans by being here."

June's eyes widen. "No, no. This is *your* house. I'm the imposition. I'll go tomorrow. If the storm doesn't–"

"We'll take the night and figure things out tomorrow. Okay? I'm not going to have you driving if the roads aren't safe. And who knows if you're even going to be able to get out of here tomorrow." I say, glancing out the window. The snow is starting to come in sheets. Aggressive and fast. I don't say it, but I think we're going to be stuck here. Even if one of us wanted to leave. "Listen, the house is huge. If you take the west wing, we can take the east and it'll be like we're here on our own accord without getting in each other's way."

She looks away shyly. "You sure? I already feel bad about being here, I don't want to–"

"Why? You need somewhere to go," I say.

June sighs. "I know, but it's..." She doesn't finish her thought. Something's behind her words. Maybe something to do with her losing her job. Or something else. I wouldn't be able to guess and I'm certainly not going to press her. We don't have that kind of relationship.

Before I can respond, Piper rushes into the room, screaming, "*Frozen*! Let's watch *Frozen*!"

I laugh, "Sounds like a perfect movie for the weather."

Piper leaps into my arms. Amazing what a long car ride and a nap can do for a child's morale.

"Yes, I love that," June says with a cheerful grin, the concern and tension of the conversation fading without question. "Now, Piper, I know you don't like fish. So... how about some chicken nuggets with your potatoes."

Piper claps her hands excitedly. "Yes, yes, yes!"

"June, please, you relax, I'll make the chicken nuggets," I protest, putting Piper down and letting her scurry back to the family room.

"You were just driving. Why don't you two relax, start the movie, and I'll have dinner ready in a jiff?" June asks with a gentle smile. I imagine this is the smile she gives to all the children she works with, the one that encourages them to follow her plan in a soft and loving way.

I already feel bad that the wires are getting crossed. If we're both going to be here, I don't want June to feel beholden to spending time with Piper or taking care of her. But I can't refuse a meal right now. Or a little help.

Maybe it will be good to have June around.

"Okay," I say quietly and nod my head. "Thank you, June."

"Don't mention it," she says.

I start to walk out of the room but stop when a thought suddenly crosses my mind. "And June?"

"Yes, Jarred?"

I lick my lower lip and take a measured breath. "Could you not tell Keifer about this? I'm kind of going off the grid for a bit and I don't want anyone to know we're out here. So, I can just focus on Pipes. You know?"

June giggles. "Don't worry. Secret's safe with me."

My eyes catch on the knot of her auburn hair on top of her head. I don't know if she's been this... vulnerable looking in front of me in a long time. Of course, when we were all kids, Keifer and June would have playdates and sleepovers and she'd be running around in her pajamas. I can't remember the last time I saw her like this, though. And it's impossible for me not to take in the way her shorts have bunched up around her waist, riding up to expose more of her pale thigh.

Shake it off, Jarred. This is June we're talking about. I tear my eyes away from her and bid her, "Thanks," as I go to join Piper in the family room.

It might not be as easy to avoid June as I think.

5

——————

JUNE

I stand at the front window and stare at the yard outside the cabin. The landscape is completely white. The drifts are so high that the cars are covered almost entirely. I haven't seen a snowstorm like this in years. Years and years. Lake Michigan no doubt made the impact even worse. And it's so cold that there's no way that it's going to start melting today.

We're stuck. Well and truly.

It's not that Jarred was an unwelcome sight. It was just so utterly unexpected. I don't think I've been able to process it, even after a good night's sleep.

Jarred is the Hawthorn boy I've spent the least amount of time with. He was always Keifer's older brother, even with the relatively small three-year gap. Always onto the next thing, the next phase of his life. And even though we see each other most Sunday nights for the Hawthorn family dinner, we don't have a lot to talk about. Jarred always seems like he has something on his mind. I talk to Piper more than Jarred.

Maybe this will be a good opportunity for us to get to know each other a little better.

"Morning."

Speak of the devil. Jarred walks into the family room, and when I see him, I have to hold my breath. He's wearing a T-shirt and a pair of sweatpants. I don't think I've ever seen him wear something like that. I can make out the outline of his dick in his crotch; I jerk my eyes away. I hope he didn't see me staring. "Good morning. Don't know if you like tea, but there's some more hot water in the kettle," I say, indicating with my mug of tea.

Jarred shakes his head. "More of a coffee person myself."

Fuck, I should have made some coffee.

"You sleep okay?" Jarred asks.

"Like a baby, honestly," I say with a smile. "Something about hearing the weather outside and knowing I'm safe and snug makes me feel like I'm wrapped up like a baby."

Jarred chuckles. "That's funny. I get that."

"How about you?"

He clears his throat. "Oh fine. I think it'll take me a couple days to get acclimated to... chilling out."

"Totally."

Jarred walks over to the space beside me and looks out at the yard. "Holy shit," he mutters and then jerks his head over his shoulder. "Sorry, always have to check for Piper."

I chuckle. "I get it."

"Right, of course you do."

I feel him wanting to ask me what happened, just like Keifer tried. But if I'm not telling Keifer, I'm certainly *not* telling Jarred. That would be insane.

"Well, we're most definitely stuck here," Jarred says with a sigh.

"Unless you've got snowmobiles out back then, yeah, I think we are."

Jarred doesn't reply. He runs a hand back through his nearly shoulder-length blonde hair, tousling it through his fingers. "I feel bad we surprised you here, June."

"This is literally your house, Jarred, I–"

"You know that doesn't matter. Keifer offered it to you to give you some peace and quiet and a roof and... well, I know how that feels. Needing the peace and quiet."

I chew on my lower lip. "Can be hard to get with a little one around, huh?"

Jarred tilts his head back and forth. "Sure, sometimes. But Piper's a good kid. Easy. For the most part."

"Yeah, but when it's just..." I trail off. I decide against saying what I was originally about to. *When it's just you.* I'm sure he thinks about that all the time. He doesn't need his kid brother's best friend to remind him of that. "Kids are hard even if they're good."

Jarred smiles to himself, gaze falling to the floor. "Sure. I guess so. All the worrying can definitely get to me. Especially now that she's at school."

"Hello!"

Jarred and I turn around to find Piper standing at the top of the stairs. She's wearing an adorable pajama set decorated with stars and moons, grinning from ear to ear.

"Good morning, Pipes!" Jarred calls up to her.

"Good..." Piper stretches her arms up to the sky. "...morning."

I laugh. "Big stretch, huh?"

Piper sighs contentedly as she comes down the stairs. She pushes herself between us to look outside. "Whoa... look at all that snow! Do you wanna build a snowman, daddy?"

"Piper, the snow is higher than you!" Jarred says,

stroking her head softly. "We might have to wait for it to melt a little or else I'll lose you."

She crosses her arms and harrumphs. "I'm hungry."

"Well, it's a snow day. I think that calls for something special," I say to brighten her mood.

Piper looks at me, her big green eyes glittering. "What kind of special?"

"Well, it'd be up to your daddy of course. But..." I wiggle my shoulders back and forth, thinking. "Pancakes? With chocolate chips? There might even be some whipped cream in the fridge. We'll have to check." I'm being the worst kind of person right now. Sugaring up someone else's kid? That's a big no-no. I can't help it, though. She's too adorable.

"Can I help?" Piper asks eagerly.

"Of course!" I reply. "I need a helper!"

"June, seriously, you don't have to... you know," Jarred says, waving his hand toward me.

I hope I haven't overstepped a boundary he's set. I'm not trying to get involved or somehow undermine him. But it would be way more fun for me to spend time with Piper than just alone in the west wing. "I don't mind! Really. I mean, as long as it's okay with you."

Jarred hesitates. He looks at Piper and then looks at me and shrugs. "Sure."

Not as enthusiastic as I'd hope, but a permission is a permission, nonetheless. I smile at him thankful and then announce, "Last one to the kitchen is a rotten egg!"

Piper hops to attention and sprints out of the room. I laugh and walk slowly after her. "Works *every* time."

Jarred laughs too. "I'll have to keep that one in my back pocket."

"I've got plenty of tricks you can have," I call over my shoulder.

After all, someone should use them.

———

"Okay, now for the finishing touch..." I say and walk over to where Piper is sitting at the kitchen table, shaking the whipped cream as I go.

Piper claps her hands together. She's already had plenty of chocolate chips and is bubbling with sugar, but hey. We're trapped inside at least for the day. She deserves all the fun we can give her. I spray the whipped cream onto her pancake. "Smiley face for the lady."

She giggles excitedly. "Give one to daddy too!"

Jarred has opted out of the pancake experience. He's made himself a bowl of oatmeal with berries and a cup of coffee. "None for me, thank you!"

"But Daddy..." Piper whines, her lower lip pouting outward.

Jarred sighs. "You know I can't resist the lower lip pout."

I laugh. "It's that easy with you?"

"Have you seen her? She's adorable!" Jarred announces.

"Give him a smiley face, June!"

I eye Jarred. "Smiley face for the gentleman?"

He rolls his eyes. "I guess."

I chuckle and put a small smiley face on his bowl of oatmeal. This feels like the way things used to be. Jarred always the reluctant but unwilling-to-disappoint recipient of the antics of Keifer and me, like when he would know that we were waiting around the corner to scare him and still act surprised, even if he did roll his eyes at us.

"Alright, everyone eat!" I announce, taking my seat on the other side of Piper, facing Jarred.

Piper eats her pancake haphazardly, taking bites from the pancake as it hangs from her fork. I offer to cut it for her, but Jarred shakes his head. "She likes to do it that way."

I giggle. Kids all have their own weird quirks. I like learning Piper's. At family dinners, she's just as charming, but her time is often monopolized by her grandfather, Ash, and Ash's new wife, Rye. Now, she's coming into her own, developing her personality and learning what she likes. This is an unexpected benefit of being stuck together.

"How long were you guys planning on staying?"

Jarred finishes a spoonful of oatmeal and then glances at Piper. "Probably just a long weekend. Although, that depends on what happens with the snow."

"Sure. Could be days... could be weeks..."

"Weeks?!" Piper asks in horror.

"No, no, I'm just kidding. They'll get a plow out here when they can."

Jarred clicks his tongue. "That reminds me, I have to get in touch with the plow company. Since this is private property, the county doesn't do the driveway. Fuuuhhhdge. Fudge."

I eye him. "That was a close one."

He puts his finger to his lips and shushes me with a smile.

"When do you think they'll be able to get out here?" I ask, cutting a piece of pancake.

"Depends. They make their own hours and sometimes they can be finnicky so. Hopefully, sooner rather than later, I guess."

I have to admit, thinking about being in this house for two weeks by myself is a daunting task. Piper and Jarred being here for even just a few days brings me relief I didn't know I needed. A huge house by myself in the middle of nowhere is a horror movie recipe.

"What were you going to do today, June?" Jarred asks, scrolling through contacts on his phone.

I swallow. "Well. Probably do a little bit of job hunting. Some television. Some reading. You know. Very busy. Very important."

Jarred chuckles. "Definitely." He dials a phone number and puts it to his ear.

"Daddy, no phones at the table," Piper complains.

"Just a quick call. Promise…"

We all wait. I can hear the busy tone from across the table. Jarred pulls the phone away from his ear and looks at it. "I'm going to have to keep calling, I guess."

Piper glares at him.

"Later," Jarred reassures. "Promise. After breakfast."

Her wariness is replaced with a smile, and she returns to her pancake.

The table is quiet for a bit, besides the sounds of us eating. I don't know what else to say. There's nothing for Jarred and me to catch up on besides the immediate circumstances. We don't really share any interests or have any gossip to share. Nothing we can shoot the shit about. Piper's the only thing that's making this even slightly bearable right now.

The silence is eventually interrupted by a quiet humming. I frown, first looking to Jarred. He seems nonplussed. Then, I look to Piper. It's clearly coming from her little lips, a thoughtless tune that comes and goes when she takes a bite of pancake.

"She does that when she's enjoying her meal," Jarred says.

I've never heard her do that, even after all the dinners. Perhaps she hasn't really enjoyed any of them quite as much as my chocolate chip pancakes. I smile smugly, "The power of the whipped cream."

Jarred laughs and looks at Piper; it's clear how much he adores her. The love in his eyes. "Is it good, Pipes?"

"Mmm!" she hums and nods.

We both laugh. Moments like these with the kids I've worked with over the years, with Piper, always remind me of the future I hope is in store for me. Although, I don't usually have a man sitting across from me. Now, I can really get the full picture.

A quiet winter morning breakfast with my daughter and husband. That's an image I could live in for a long time. Not with Jarred and Piper, obviously. But if I let my mind linger on the idea of Jarred for just a minute...no. It wouldn't make sense. Besides the fact we're practically family, we're just too different. He deals with facts and figures. I deal with crayons and glue. I look at him and I see a grown-up. I still feel like a kid compared to him, even though we're only a few years apart.

He's just a placeholder for now. After all, I'm good at playing pretend.

6

———————

JARRED

Two days and the snow hasn't budged an inch. We're on a waitlist for getting plowed out. Probably won't get to us until Tuesday. This long weekend is looking to be a bit longer than I anticipated.

Admittedly, I haven't known what to do with June being here. Don't get me wrong, she's lovely. In most every way. I could have been stuck with someone not nearly as comfortable being around a three-year-old. Someone not nearly as friendly or funny.

But June is *Keifer's*. Not romantically, that's always been clear. But as a family, we all have our default people, the ones who are like family, but would never hang out with the family without us being there. And that's who June is for Keifer.

I've known her... well, most of my life at this point, which is hard to believe. She's my littlest brother's best friend. And yet, I've never spent any one-on-one time with her.

I'm now realizing there is a good reason for that.

June is... stunning. This in and of itself isn't news. It's just seeing her in this new light, every light, morning, noon, and night. Well, it's a whole new side of June completely.

I should have known from the moment I saw her bare legs when she waltzed out into the winter night to greet me, thinking I was Keifer, that this would be a problem. I think I've been doing okay. I don't stare for too long or extend conversations longer than they need to go. I would be able to get through this long, *long* weekend and move on from the idea of June all together.

Except for the small issue of my daughter.

It's Sunday afternoon. And there is more snow falling outside, except now it's soft. Powdered sugar, drifting through the air. Piper is sitting on a window seat, staring out at how it floats down. "Look, look, it's snowing!"

I look away briefly from the television that's playing a football game and smile at her. "I see, Pipes."

Of course, June rushes over and joins Piper on the window seat. She rushes over to Piper if she so much as sneezes. She always makes it clear she doesn't want to overstep, but always ends up overstepping. At least in my eyes. Not that I mind, but still. "Look at the snowflakes! Did you know every snowflake is unique, Piper?"

"*Every* one?"

"Yes!" June announces excitedly. "*Every* one. Just like people. We're all unique too. That's how no one is as cute as you."

Piper giggles and looks up at June with admiration.

I get a pang in my heart. She never gets this. Piper is surrounded by love all the time. Her uncles, her grandfather. But she's never had a woman in her life to turn to. Her mother's so far out of the picture. I sometimes wonder if

Piper will even have memories of her when she grows up. It breaks my heart. She's such a sweet, tender little girl.

"I wish I could go outside..." Piper laments for the five hundredth time in these past two days.

"I know, I know," June sighs. "Tomorrow, hopefully. But the snow is just too high right now."

They are quiet again. I can't seem to return my eyes to the game; the image of Piper and June together is so... interesting. Piper's light blonde hair and June's brownish red contrast beside one another.

Slowly, June leans forward and breathes on the glass window, causing it to condensate. Then, she traces her fingers through it, writing P-I-P-E-R. "Do you know what that says?"

Piper gets up onto her knees with a giggle. "*Piper!*"

"Mhm. You got it."

Piper leans forward and does this same. Instead of writing a word, she draws a crinkly looking heart.

"That's a pretty heart, Piper."

June is filled with an eternal positivity. It's not annoying, though, and those kinds of people usually annoy me. She always seems to see something good or beautiful in what's happening. It's staved off Piper's cabin fever immensely. Each thing has been something to discover, from the creaking floorboards that June compared to old piano keys to the stuffed pheasant on the wall that used to scare Piper, but now that June has given him a funny voice, makes her laugh.

"Write, Piper and June. With a gap," Piper asks.

Oh no.

June does as the little girl asks and, once she's finished, Piper draws a heart between both names. "Piper 'heart'

June". It's not hard for children to fall in love with people and things. Just recently, I've seen how Piper has fallen head over heels with Rye, her new grandmother, ostensibly. It didn't take long.

"Aw, Piper. Thank you. June 'hearts' Piper too!" June says and then tickles Piper's belly.

Piper lets out a ream of laughter, throwing her head back, blonde curls falling back.

"Hey, listen," June says to Piper and then leans in and whispers in her ear.

"Are you two talking about me?" I ask with a half-smile.

Piper laughs. "No, Daddy! No!"

"Promise," June adds and then goes back to whispering. "Did you get all that?" she asks Piper at full volume when she's done.

Piper nods firmly and then jumps off the bench, rushes over to where I am on the couch, and leaps onto my lap.

"Oh, whoa!" I wheeze. "Have you gotten bigger in the past two days or is that my imagination?"

Piper laughs and grabs onto my T-shirt. "Daddy..."

I wrap my arms around her. I don't want her to get bigger. She's already too big for her own good. I want her small forever so I can hold her and protect her.

"I have a question," Piper says, dipping her chin down bashfully.

I smile and run my hand through her hair. "What is it, pumpkin?"

She leans into my ear and presses her lips to it. When she starts to whisper, I jolt away. "Whoa, whoa, you're too close! I can't hear what you're saying! All I hear is shkshskshsk."

Piper laughs and then tries again, this time an appropriate distance away. "Can June and I see if we can catch snowflakes on the front porch?"

I chuckle, glancing over at June. She's sitting on the window bench, swinging her legs, looking at us and waiting. As soon as my eyes meet hers, she looks away, back outside at the flurrying snow. I turn back to Piper. "Sure, honey. But I don't want you to be disappointed if you can't get any."

"I won't, I won't. We just want to *try*," Piper says, spreading her hands emphatically.

I twist my lips together, pretending to think. "Well..."

"Please, Daddy, please!"

"You have to wear a coat..."

"I will!"

"And when you lean your head back you have to go 'ahhhhhhhhhhh'," I continue.

June giggles. It fills me with a little bit of warmth. *What's going on with me?*

"I will! See? Ahhhhhh..." Piper demonstrates with a wide mouth.

"Perfect! You've got it. Okay, I guess you can go try and catch a snowflake."

Piper celebrates, wiggling her whole body. "Yay! Did you hear, June? Daddy said yes!"

"I did hear! That's very exciting." June grins. "I also heard that we have to put our coats on first so..."

The girls rush into the front hall to put on their winter apparel. I stay in front of the game for a second, but I can't resist going to watch. I follow them into the hall and, once they're ready, open the door for them. The front stoop has been protected by the overhang with only a few inches of snow compared to the three feet everywhere else. And when the wind blows just right, snowflakes dance under the overhang.

"Okey dokey, you ready?" June asks Piper.

Piper nods giddily and toddles out onto the stoop in her big fluffy jacket and clunky boots.

"Okay, Piper, let's do as Daddy said, hm?" June says encouragingly.

I don't want to admit that June calling me "daddy" even in such a pure and friendly context makes me feel funny. But there it is.

Piper tilts her head back, sticks out her tongue, and says, "Ahhhhhh!" June does too. They wait a moment.

"I got one!" June announces happily.

Piper harrumphs, "I didn't."

I haven't closed the door behind them. They're too cute to watch.

"Here," June lifts Piper off the ground and places her on her hip. "Try from up here."

Piper loops her arms around June's neck. I hold back a sigh. They try again and only a few seconds later, Piper squeals excitedly. "I got one, I got one!"

"You did? Fantastic!" June exclaims. "One more before we go back inside."

I wonder why June lost her job. She seems... too good at it. I can't imagine why a family would want to get rid of such a positive energy. Someone so willing to make the little things in life grand and wonderful. Those of us with a lot of money need that. We can get caught up in being able to have everything that it feels like nothing really matters.

With June around, it's the little things that matter. And that's just what Piper needs.

I wave the thought away. I can't be having these thoughts about *Juniper Reed*. She's been implicitly off-limits since she was five years old, and she came to Keifer's birthday party and had two huge slices of cake. There's too much history wrapped up in that. Plus, I'm not sure I'll ever let someone in like that again. Not after the betrayal I've faced.

It's hard, though, to watch how good she is with Piper and not wonder: *what if?*

7

———

JUNE

Finally, we're able to be out in the snow. Piper has been begging ever since it started. But it was too high and too fresh to let her tromp around it.

Now, Tuesday, she breaks free from the house in her full winter getup. Hat, gloves, snowpants. The works.

"Slow down, Piper! Be careful!" Jarred calls after her, having only just stepped onto the front stoop.

Neither of us can move quite as quickly. We're wearing full body snowsuits that were stored in one of the closets, the type used for skiing or snowboarding. In this case, though, the boys mostly use them for riding the snow mobiles that are stored out back. I'm wearing Keifer's; the cuffs of the legs and arms are rolled up since they're so long.

"I feel like a big purple marshmallow," I murmur.

Jarred laughs. "You don't look like a marshmallow."

I roll my eyes. He's being nice. "Thank you."

"Look, guys, look at me!"

We both watch Piper as she runs and leaps into a snow-bank, the snow swallowing her softly, soundlessly. It's both ominous and adorable.

"Wait up, wait up! I want to try!" Jarred announces and runs after her.

In just these four days, Jarred has changed. He's not the same Jarred I see at Sunday dinners. Usually, he's so serious about everything. He's got work on his mind or Piper to pay attention too. Always distracted. Now, he's managed to leave some of that behind and just... enjoy the moment.

We've talked more the past few days than we have in probably years. At family dinners, it's easy for us to just be part of a group conversation. Here, it's just us. And Piper, of course. She honestly makes it easier for Jarred and me to have a rapport. Now, it's nothing deep, mostly bantering, but who knows? Maybe that'll change.

Jarred has joined Piper leaping into the snowbank, but when he does it, he lets out a loud, "Oof!" Piper laughs in response.

I lean on one of the columns holding up the overhang. "The bigger they are, the harder they fall, Jarred!"

He doesn't respond with words, just a long groan.

Piper gets up and starts to pull on Jarred's hand, but with all her three-year-old effort she can't get him to budge an inch. "June! Help!"

I rush over, tromping through the snow as quick as I can, and assess the damage. Jarred is snug in the snowbank, unhurt, but definitely needs a hand. "Leave me!" he says melodramatically. "Go on without me! Don't forget me!"

"Okay, drama queen," I tease. "Give me your hand."

Jarred extends a gloved hand toward me and I take it. With our grips tight, I yank him up out of the snowbank to his feet. "Thank you," he says, clutching his heart. "I thought I was stuck there forever."

"*Daddy...*" Piper rolls her eyes, hands on her hips. "No, you didn't."

"Yikes, she clocked you," I say to Jarred.

He shakes his head with a sigh, "She always does. That feminine intuition or whatever."

I laugh. A three-year-old with feminine intuition? Please. "Right, it wasn't at all the heart-clutching melodrama of it all... she used her *feminine intuition*."

Jarred scoffs, "Don't be jealous of my acting abilities."

"Oh, I'm not. Trust me."

Jarred bites on his tongue, a smile on his lips. We could go back and forth like this for a while. I know we shouldn't. Bantering and teasing... well, that's what gets me into trouble when it comes to guys. I've never shook the idea of "He teases you because he likes you" that my mother instilled in me as a girl. That's perhaps why Keifer has always been squarely in the friendzone. He's just too nice to me. We give each other shit *now*, but as kids, he was just the sweetest little boy on the playground.

With Jarred, it's different, now that we're gaining a one-on-one relationship, the fact that so much of it is joking and teasing leads me toward... other feelings I know I shouldn't be having.

Jarred is objectively handsome. Unlike the rest of the Hawthorn boys, he wears his hair long. And it's obviously very well cared for. Thick and shiny. I'd love to run my hands through it. Just once. To see.

"Let's make a snowman!" Piper announces.

"Okay, you pick the spot, Pipes," Jarred instructs.

She finds a nice spot for the snowman near a fir tree. "We need materials now. A hat and arms and a carrot for a nose and–"

"How about you two get started on the body and I'll go pick out some materials from inside?" I ask.

"Okay!" she says enthusiastically and then starts packing snow together on the ground.

Jarred smiles at me. "Thanks, June."

Thanks, June. Who does he think he is, saying my name like that? "Don't mention it," I reply. Then, I head back inside.

I'm determined to leave the snowsuit on. After all, it took me about five minutes to get into the damn thing. But getting my boots off to go in the house proves to be tricky. It takes me awhile to get all the materials as I'm shuffling around and overheating in my snowsuit, but I manage. I have a carrot, buttons, a hat, and a scarf.

By the time I make it back outside, Jarred and Piper are already rolling the midsection of the body. They're rolling the big snowball together, tromping through the snow. Piper has on a big grin, her cheeks red from the cold. I have to stand and watch them for a minute.

They're a cute pair. Two peas in a pod. Jarred and Piper, Piper and Jarred. I remember when I found out that Jarred and his wife at the time were having a baby. How excited he was. He was fixated on Piper before he even met her. Every conversation he was a part of was about babies, about kids, about his wife's pregnancy. Eventually, his brothers put an embargo on him talking because they were so annoyed by it. But not me. His thrill and excitement were so heartening. I was in my early twenties, had just been through a breakup, and could not fathom a man being loving.

And then I watched Jarred become a dad. And that gave me a little hope. I've never told him that.

Piper stops and lets Jarred roll the snowball a bit further without her. Jarred stops and turns around with his hands on his hips. I can't make out the words, but I can hear the tone of his voice. He's teasing her for having stopped.

And then there's Piper's beautiful, bubbly giggle.

Jarred approaches her slowly and then snatches her up in his arms, giving her kisses and throwing her over his shoulder like a sack of potatoes.

He's a good dad.

When the moment finishes, I finally speak up. "You two work fast!"

"No!" Jarred calls back. "You're just very slow!"

I flush. I love his teases. They're so harmless. Admittedly, I was afraid to be in a house, just me and a grown man, even if it is Keifer's brother. I wasn't sure how safe I'd feel. But Jarred hasn't made me worry at all. He's much more preoccupied with Piper anyways.

I rush out to join them and help Jarred lift the midsection onto the lower part of the snowman's body while Piper snaps some small branches off a tree to serve as arms. She sticks them in triumphantly.

"There!" I say, dusting my hands together. "All done!"

"No, silly! We still need a head!"

"Ah! Yes. You're right."

"So silly, June," Jarred says, shaking his head.

I give him a look, a private smile of sorts, and then immediately look away. My instincts are getting stronger each moment we spend together. I couldn't even help the flirtatious smile I gave him. Hopefully, he's not reading into it. Hopefully, he looks at me and only sees a thirteen-year-old with braces.

Keifer would kill me if anything ever happened between me and one of his brothers. I've never even thought about it anyway. I'm already a part of the Hawthorn family. I don't need to marry into it.

June, stop it. You're barely flirting with Jarred; you can't be thinking about marriage.

I'm not thinking about marriage, but I am at an age where my mind is starting to stray that way. My clock is going to start ticking louder in the coming years. And being that I haven't been in a relationship in three years, I'm starting to wonder if I'll ever date again. Best not start fantasizing about my best friend's brother.

"Okay, Piper! The head!" Jarred announces.

We let Piper make the head on her own, since it's smaller. She does a phenomenal job, but she can't quite pick it up, so Jarred picks it up and lets her guide it up to the top of the snowman with her hands. "Good job, Pipes," Jarred says. "It's really coming together."

"Now, for the real fun," I say, holding up the carrot.

Jarred lifts Piper up so she can decorate the face. She easily makes a jovial looking snowman with big button eyes, a bulbous carrot nose, and a curved twig to serve as the mouth. As she does this, I wrap a scarf around the snowman's neck. Then, when all of this is done, I hand her a yellow furry beanie I found in one of the closets. "The finishing touch!"

Piper puts the hat on the snowman's head, tamping it down so it stays. We all take a step back to admire our creation. It's one of the funniest snowmen I've ever seen. Like a tacky dad from the seventies. "What are we going to name him?" Jarred asks Piper, adjusting her on his hips.

She thinks; she has the cutest thinking face. Her tongue comes out over her upper lip, and she looks up into the sky. Sometimes, she taps her chin with her finger. It's adorable. "Freddy!"

Jarred raises his eyebrows. "That's a great name for a snowman! Where'd you come up with that?"

Piper shrugs. "Just like it."

"You heard her! The woman likes what the woman likes," I say. "Freddy the Snowman. I love it."

Jarred and I exchange a smile before he says, "Okay, Piper, maybe we should go back in and–"

"Noooo, I'm not ready to go back inside."

"I can stay out here with her if you want," I say.

Jarred hesitates. "Uh. No, June, that's okay."

I chew on the inside of my cheek. I am an overachiever when it comes to kids. I know I've been pushing Jarred's boundaries when it comes to how much I'm helping. I even offered to give her a bath last night. He looked at me like a crazy person for that one.

I can't help it. Kids love so bigly and so easily. I like to be around that energy as much as possible.

But I do know that treading on the territory of a mom or dad can be dangerous. And when it comes to Jarred, his territory is even more well-marked. He's superbly protective of Piper and his bond with her.

"But, Daddy, I don't want to go in yet!" Piper wails, on the verge of tears.

"Right, right, I get it," he mumbles, his dad voice fading.

I can't imagine how hard it must be for him to be parenting Piper on his own. Not to mention being the chief of something at Hawthorn (I've never had a mind for business and never really remember the titles). He makes it work, though. And she loves him to absolute pieces. I bet people offering help can seem like he's not doing good enough.

Instead of interrupting with words, I fall onto my back, splayed out onto the ground. This impromptu gesture sends Piper into a laugh. "June, what are you doing?"

"Snow angel," I say and then start to move my limbs

back and forth through the snow. "Haven't you ever done one?"

Somehow, she squirms out of Jarred's arms to the ground and joins me in the snow, waving her arms back and forth. "I'm flying! I'm flying like an angel!"

"Yes, me too!" I reply. "Here we go!"

"Daddy, come fly with us."

Jarred sighs and then tromps through the snow to his own spot. He lays back but doesn't move his arms.

"Just move your arms up and down and your legs back and forth," Piper instructs, still making her own angel.

He starts to do so. The sound of the snow shifting is all I can hear for a bit. We're all laying on our backs, staring into the sky. "Flying". Funnily enough, the longer I stare into the sky, the more it really does feel like flying. The sky is so big, wide, and deep. It makes life feel endless, limitless. I forget about my problems back in Chicago, forget that I'm here because Keifer's doing me a favor. And instead, I focus on what's right here. The sky. And little Piper. And Jarred.

Why does that feel so full of possibility?

8

———

JARRED

"How about a game of Candyland?"

"Mmgh."

"Monopoly."

"*Mmgh.*"

"Chutes and Ladders?"

"Mmgh!"

I sigh and look up from the cabinet of games. Piper is sitting on the sofa with her arms crossed and an angry look on her face. "Piper, why don't you come down here and pick out a game?"

"I don't want to pick out a game."

I turn away from her and roll my eyes so she doesn't see. Sometimes, when she gets hard to please, I can't help but take a moment. I understand she's getting bored. The plowing company's pushed back their arrival already by two extra days. I'm hoping they'll show up tomorrow, Friday, and then we can head out Saturday morning. But for now, we're stuck.

"I want to play with June," she adds loudly.

I close my eyes. "Piper, I've already explained." I get up

and sit next to her on the couch. "Come here," I say and wrap my arm around her. She props her little feet up on my thigh and droops her head into my side. "June needs her alone time. She's showering and resting and–"

"But *you* don't need alone time," she retorts.

I chuckle. Of course, I do, but she doesn't know that yet. She's still at an age where boundaries are nearly incomprehensible. "But I'm your dad, sweet pea. We're supposed to spend lots and lots of time together."

Piper crosses her arms and looks away from me. "June's been spending lots and lots of time with me."

I nod. "That's true."

"So, doesn't she like me anymore?"

My jaw tightens. I'm always worried that Piper already knows abandonment, somewhere deep inside her. I always worry that she somehow remembers the moment her mother said, "I can't take this anymore," while Piper threw noodles on the ground from her highchair. Is that why she's feeling so strongly about June taking a break? "You and June are like good friends, Piper," I say softly, taking her foot in my hand tenderly. "Friends don't hang out together all the time. They need breaks."

"I don't need a break, though," she mopes.

"Don't you want to spend time with me?" I ask, attempting to smile.

She sighs, wrapping an arm around my stomach. "I always spend time with you. You're my daddy."

Somehow, that cuts deep. She's over it. I'm just her dad. She needs more than me. I've known this ever since Meredith left. That there'd be this hole. She's been starting to see it. And having June here... it's just confused her even more.

"Pssst."

Piper and I both jump and look around.

"Pssst. Up here."

We look up to the balcony. June is crouched down between the spindles of the balustrade, looking at us like she has a secret.

"June!" Piper shouts.

"Shhh!" June hushes her and then extends her arm to wave us up the stairs.

I'm confused, but Piper catches on right away, jumping out of my arms and scurrying up the stairs to the upper west wing of the house. As soon as she's up there, June darts into the hallway out of sight and Piper follows her. I sit there like an idiot in complete bewilderment. What the fuck just happened?

Better go find out.

I get to my feet and race to catch up with them. "Guys, wait!" I call out, but when I get into the hall, there's no one to be seen. "Guys?"

I hear some tittering laughter and another "Shh!" coming from June's room at the end of the hall, the one across from the deer head. I've never liked the hunting décor around the house, but it came with all the furniture and at the time, me and the other Hawthorn boys weren't really interested in decorating. So stuffed deer head it was and has been ever since. I tiptoe down the hallway as silent as a mouse. I'm not sure what we're being quiet about, but I'm not going to ruin the game.

Finally, I get to the door of June's room. My jaw drops. Before me is the greatest pillow and blanket fort I've ever seen. I'm not sure how she constructed it or where she got all the materials. There are twinkling lights arranged around the room, making it look like the coziest spot-on earth. The blankets create a canopy over the bounty of pillows. I know that if I laid in them, I would fall right to sleep.

Piper is already hopping into the fort and curling up around a pillow. She looks as gleeful as can be.

"Wow, June, this is... wow," I say, blinking because I can't quite believe my eyes.

"Look, Daddy! *Frozen!*" Piper points to the television across the room where, sure enough *Frozen* is ready to go.

"*Frozen? Again?*" I ask with a terror-filled look to June. We've already watched it three times and we've been here under a week.

"Don't worry," June says with a chuckle. "It's the sequel."

I wipe my brow playfully. "Fewf! That was a close one."

"Daddy! June! Come sit!"

June's room is cozy, but still spacious. Her bed, though, is only a queen. It will be a tight fit. But with Piper tucked right at the center of the fort, maybe it won't be so bad. June and I get into the bed on either side of Piper. The mattress sinks beneath our weight. I can feel gravity pulling us toward the middle of the bed just the slightest bit. But I ignore it.

"Popcorn?" June produces a bowl of popcorn from the nightstand.

"Mmm!" Piper exclaims and takes the big bowl, tucking it onto her lap.

"Hey! You have to share that!" I cry out, taking a big handful.

Her eyes go big, brow tightening. "Daddy! That's too much!"

We fuss over the popcorn as June starts the movie. "Okay, you two, there's plenty of popcorn. Relax!" she says, tapping Piper's shoulder admonishingly.

The three of us are swept away into the comfort of the fortress. It's so easy to relax in here. The rest of the world, the cold, my job, the stress, all disappears while we're all snug in June's bed.

I try my best to focus on the movie, but it becomes difficult with June in my periphery. Her hair is wet and pulled back into a ponytail and she's not wearing any makeup. Yet, she glows in a way I've never seen. The twinkle lights only heighten this. Her skin looks warm and soft. Her lips are twinged in a permanent, serene smile.

I'll admit it. I want to kiss her.

I won't, obviously. Especially not with my daughter between us. But I won't. Ever. There's too much baggage wrapped up in that.

I can live on a daydream of her. Just a little one. The only reason I'm even thinking about her like this is because of exposure. Who wouldn't start falling for their brother's best friend just a little bit when they're trapped in a cabin with them *and* they're good with your motherless child? Exactly. No one.

About half an hour into the movie, June leans over to Piper and whispers, "How do you feel about some hot chocolate?"

"Mmm..."

"You're going to have a mouthful of cavities after this trip," I say wryly.

June looks at me worriedly. "I'm sorry, I should have asked if she can–"

"No, no! I'm not going to deny my daughter hot chocolate at a time like this," I chuckle.

She breathes a sigh of relief. "Okay, good." June gets up from the bed and goes to the door. "Do you want some, Jarred?"

I glance around at the surroundings. "Yeah, actually. I think I might have some."

"Marshmallows? Whipped cream? Candy cane?"

"The works," I say.

June smiles at me; it reminds me of the way my mom smiled at me when I was a kid. Like I'm dear and small and deserve to be taken care of. God, first I want to kiss this woman and now I'm comparing her to my mother? What kind of Freudian shit is this?

As soon as June disappears out the door, I realize how rude I'm being. She created this whole tent situation for Piper and now is going to make us hot chocolate and I'm just kicking back watching *Frozen* 2. That's not the man I've been raised to be. "Pipes, I'm gonna go help June. I'll be right back."

"Okay," she replies, her eyes glued to the screen.

I slip out of the room quietly and go down to the kitchen where June is standing at the stove, heating up some milk. When she sees me, she seems surprised. "Do you need to change your order?"

I wince at that comment. I know she's joking, but it's just adding more to the idea that I'm using her. "No, I just came down to thank you. For everything."

"Oh," she says and waves her hand as if it's nothing. "I found a closet of blankets and thought it'd be fun. No big deal."

"June, it *is* a big deal. It's really special and thoughtful," I reply. "Piper doesn't get a lot of moments like that."

June focuses on stirring the milk. I can tell she isn't sure what to say. "She gets tons of moments like that. Are you kidding, Jarred?" She shuts off the burner and then looks at me. "You're a great dad. And your brothers and dad do everything they can and–"

"Yes, but it's not like having a woman around. It's different."

By the way her face changes, I can tell I've said too much. Her eyes widen and her lips droop in shock.

"Not that–I don't mean–" I stumble through my words. "You came out here to be alone and then we showed up and you've gone above and beyond to make sure she's having fun and... Just thank you."

"I'm having a great time, Jarred. So, thank you too," June replies. Then, she goes back to making the hot chocolate, pouring the milk and spooning cocoa into three mugs.

I start to back out of the room but catch myself on the doorframe. "Can I... pay you?"

June laughs. "What?"

"It's just... it feels like you're working. You're doing so much. And I just would feel better if I could– "

"I'm not doing these things to get paid, Jarred," June snaps suddenly. Her eyes are hardened in mine. That eternal serene smile has changed into a grimace.

I swallow. "I know you're not. I just don't want you to feel used."

"I don't."

"Okay."

June's countenance changes yet again, softening. "I'm sorry. I didn't mean to snap at you."

"It's okay," I reply.

"I just–" she cuts herself off and grabs a bag of mini marshmallows. "I thought we were kind of like family. A little bit. So, this just feels like me being a part of that."

I don't reply. That breaks my heart. She's right. She is a part of the family. From what I understand, she doesn't have her own around much anymore. I just have always seen her as an extension of Keifer. Not more than that.

"I'm sorry if that's weird, I know we're not that close."

"No, it's not weird. Of course, you're family, June," I say gently.

June looks up from her work and rests her hands on the counters.

"Maybe we haven't been close over the years, but Piper's always felt close to you. And I'm feeling like we're getting closer," I say trying to inflect my words with humor and charm. The word "close" is losing all meaning.

She smiles gratefully. "Yeah. Me too."

"Forget I asked about the money thing. I just wanted to make sure that you knew how much you're appreciated. By Piper." *By me.*

"Thanks." June smiles.

The room feels warm. Everything is at ease again. I offer to help her carry the hot chocolate upstairs. When we arrive, Piper is thrilled. We all sip our cocoa carefully, nuzzling into our winter hideaway, and enjoy the movie.

As the credits roll, I realize I'm the only one still awake. June is snoring softly, her hand over her eyes. And Piper has curled into her, mouth lolling open, stained with chocolate. Together, they could be a stock image for "coziness." For "love" even.

I watch them together, burning the picture on my brain. I wish June had taken my offer and let me pay her. Because now, the boundary between us is based only on the social contract that we are proxy family. There's no emotional boundary there like employer and employee.

Which means this could get a whole lot messier.

And to be completely honest... I wouldn't mind getting messy.

9

———

JUNE

Sunday. The driveway was plowed just yesterday but it's still icy. Piper and Jarred are still here. Even though he's been anxious to get out of here, now that he can, he isn't so sure.

"Would it be so bad to stay another week?" he mused to me one evening as we were doing the dishes.

"Of course not," I replied.

"But my work–"

"Will be fine," I said.

Jarred looked at me, studied me for a long second. I was wondering if he could sense that I was working out of self-interest at this point. I didn't want Jarred and Piper to go. They'd become my companions. I couldn't imagine being in the big house by myself again.

"You're right," he said finally.

So, Piper and Jarred are going to be here nearly the rest of the week. I'm grateful. I have to wonder how this time spent together will change the way Jarred and I interact back in the "real world." The cabin doesn't feel like the real world. It's been like a private little snow globe. And I've always wanted to be trapped in a snow globe. A little colorful village ensconced in time with flurries of snow at the whim of some outside force.

That sounds like a simple life.

Piper is still asleep. Last night was a late night. We were having too much fun with a game of Monopoly that went on... and on... and on. And a little too much sugar had her bouncing off the walls until nearly midnight.

I think we can expect a late appearance from her today. I'm holed up in the balmy kitchen with a cup of tea and my computer. I'm looking through Indeed for nanny jobs. I could contact the agency I used to work for, but I don't know if I want to get involved in that racket again.

My eyes are starting to hurt from staring at the screen when I hear the clunking of wheels outside the window. I try to see what's going on through the window, but they're too frosted to see through.

I haven't seen Jarred this morning. But I can't possibly imagine what he's doing out there. I get up and throw on my coat to go see what's going on.

When I walk out the front door, I find Jarred rolling the garbage can down the long, long driveway. "What are you doing?" I call out.

"What does it look like?" he cries back over his shoulder with a smile. He looks like a Norwegian god with his long hair, set in a snowy landscape.

"You're not walking all the way down the driveway. You'll fall on your ass!"

"The trash has to get taken out, June."

I cross my arms and watch as he walks. A moment later, he skids on an ice patch, but steadies himself on the can. "Told you!"

Jarred stops a moment and looks down the sprawl of the driveway.

"Besides, we're due for more snow tonight. The garbage truck might not even come tomorrow."

Jarred huffs and runs a hand back through his hair. "What do you suggest we do, then? Drown in filth?"

I pretend to think for a moment.

"You could *help* me."

I grin devilishly. "No." And then, grab a handful of snow, ball it up, and throw it toward Jarred.

It hits him square in the chest. His jaw drops and then he looks at me. "June!"

I half-expect him to be unamused and so I start to apologize, "I know, I know, I'm childish, but–" I have to stop to dodge a bullet of white snow flying toward my face. "Ahh! Not the face!"

"All's fair in love and snowball fights, Juniper!"

I laugh loudly. "Fine! You're on!" Then, I grab a handful of snow, ready to go to war.

The last time I had a snowball fight was probably college. I never have them with the kids I work with. It's too violent and can easily get out of hand. But with a grown ass man, I'm no holds barred. Jarred and I spar quickly, lobbing balls back and forth. We're dodging, jumping, rolling away. It's a full body workout, but it doesn't feel like exercise. It's just *fun*.

Jarred doesn't even look like he's breaking a sweat. I know he runs most mornings. I can hear the treadmill running sometimes late at night too.

When he lands three snowballs in a row (one to my leg, one to my belly, one to my shoulder) I realize I'm up against a menace. "Timeout! Timeout!" I cry out, catching my breath.

Jarred listens, miraculously. He has more self-restraint than Keifer. "You okay?" he calls out from his position in one of the snowdrifts.

I stare at him for a moment and then, without a word, dart off around the house.

"That was cheap, June!" I hear him yell.

I laugh loudly. I don't care about playing dirty. I play to *win*. I scan the backyard and spot a perfect tree to hide behind. Jarred is coming, fast. I can hear his boots crunching in the snow. I make my move, concealing myself behind the tree.

"What is this, hide and seek?" he cries out when he finds I'm nowhere to be seen. His footsteps stop and then start again, stalking around the yard. "Hmmm... where could you be?"

My heart is beating fast. It's the kind of thrilling terror you have as a kid when you're playing a chase game with your mom. You know you're totally safe, but your body still produces the feeling of anxious exhilaration. Something very fun about choosing to be prey.

"Come out, come out, wherever you are..."

I gather a snowball in my hands, packing it tightly. *I'm gonna nail him.* It's going to be perfect. I'll take him completely off-guard, and he'll gasp and cry out my name in frustration. Oh, it'll be so good.

I lie in wait, listening to where his footsteps go, zigzagging through the yard. Until they abruptly stop. I swallow and widen my eyes. Fuck. Where did he go? I peek around the tree on one side. No sign of Jarred. I wind up my arm, prepared to strike, and jump out from behind the other side of the tree. "Gotcha!" I announce.

But there's no sign of Jarred. In fact, the yard is

completely empty. I drop my arm and frown. "What the fuck!"

Then, from my left, with the power of a linebacker, I'm pushed to the ground. I scream in surprise.

"No, I got *you*!" Jarred yells from his place on top of me.

I'm pinned to the snow, squirming to get up. "Let me go! Let me go!"

"Do you surrender?" he asks in a playful, roaring voice.

"I give up! I surrender! Spare me!" I say through breathless laughter.

My excitement is interrupted abruptly when I notice how Jarred has me pinned to the ground, straddling me. I'm tucked between his knees as he towers above me. His hands encircle my wrists, pinned next to my head. And his face is only a few inches from mine. The playfighting looks a lot like something else.

And I love it.

"I give up," I repeat, but I don't know if I'm still talking about our game of cat and mouse.

Jarred's eyes lock in mine. It's like he's gone somewhere else. A world where him being on top of me makes sense. And, without another word, he kisses me.

He fucking *kisses* me. His lips send fireworks through my body and blood rushes to my face. I'm no longer in the Michigan cold, but somewhere blistering with heat. My hands strain in his grasp. I want to touch him, run my hands through his hair, deepen the kiss. Maybe more. I let out a moan without thinking.

Jarred jerks backward onto his knees, breaking the kiss. "Oh my god, I'm so sorry."

I shake my head vehemently and scramble out from between his legs. "It's okay, it's okay."

"I didn't mean–"

"Me either! Me either. At all." I don't even know what we're getting at, what we're saying. But it's clear the moment is over. Permanently. My eyes catch Jarred's again, but I look away. Those blue green eyes are hypnotic. I could lose myself there. Would be a bad idea. "We should get back inside... in case Piper is up or–"

"Right, right. Totally," Jarred says and then gets to his feet.

I start to get up but pause when he offers me his hand. It'd be rude to not take it, make this moment even weirder than it already is. "Thanks," I mutter as I get to standing.

As soon as his hand falls from mine, my heart cracks. Shit. Shit, shit, shit.

I just kissed my best friend's brother. And I really enjoyed it. In fact, I'd like to do it again.

I stamp on that feeling as if it's a big, ugly bug. Feels good to quash the feeling. But unlike bugs, feelings aren't nearly as easy to kill. I can already feel it coming back to life. I'll have to ignore it for now. There is no way I can do that again. And there's definitely no way we could do any more than that. Jarred, though not as close to me as Keifer, is like a brother. All the Hawthorn boys are. Ash is like a dad to me. He's called me the daughter he's never had (although now that he and Rye are having a girl, I guess that's no longer true). Jarred and me... that would be almost incestuous.

Jarred and I brush ourselves off and then start to head inside. We are quiet at first, but I do not doubt both of our minds are loud.

"Getting warmer out," Jarred remarks.

Great. Now we're talking about the weather. "Yep. Sure is."

"Hope the snow doesn't melt too much or Piper will be bummed."

"Definitely. The slush and the mud," I reply.

We get to the back door and stamp our feet clean of snow. But just before I follow Jarred inside, I look back at the tree, at the place where we kissed. I can see the outline of the memory right there. The way that we once were. All the 'could have beens'.

It will have to stay that way. And it hurts way more than I want it too.

10

JARRED

I don't know what got into me. Just having her there under me, so beautiful and at my mercy, stirred something in me. And something in her eyes called to me.

But it was a mistake.

June and I recovered okay. The rest of yesterday was tense. June kept mostly to herself but joined us for meals. This, of course, left Piper wondering where her playmate was. I did my best to entertain her, but she's gotten so used to June being around that she's expecting it.

I didn't realize I'd have to be afraid of Piper becoming attached to someone through me. I haven't done any dating since the divorce because one of my biggest fears is falling in love with someone that Piper doesn't like. And Piper always comes first.

I don't know if I can go through that heartbreak.

But June is *not* the girl for me. We're too close to one another, even if we haven't been *close* these past few years. God, if Keifer found out... that would be cataclysmic.

This morning, though, Piper has served as a perfect

distraction. Breakfast started quietly; when Piper noticed it was snowing out, she started singing, "Let It Snow, Let It Snow, Let It Snow" on an unending loop. She doesn't know most of the lyrics, so the repetition became almost mindless. At one point, June and I exchanged a humored smile.

Leave it to Piper to make things easier.

"I know what we should do," June had said at the end of breakfast. "We should make our own perfectly unique snowflakes."

Now, I'm cleaning up the mess of breakfast while June and Piper are sitting at the kitchen table going to town with safety scissors on paper snowflakes. Scraps of paper litter the floor as if it's snowed inside.

June always has an idea for something to do. I would have run out of activities halfway through last week if it had just been me and Piper here. I'm not very crafty, like the moms on Pinterest. But she always has a craft, a recipe, a game. She can make something out of nothing.

"June, June! What do you think?" Piper cries out.

I glance over my shoulder and watch as she unfolds a snowflake. It's... hideous. But as it's the artistic work of my daughter, it's also the most beautiful paper snowflake I've ever seen.

"Wow, Piper! Look at that! You did such a nice job," June says.

Piper bounces excitedly and throws the snowflake to the side, grabbing for another sheet of paper.

This time away is working. Piper's brighter, lighter, so far away from her cares and worries. It makes me so happy. I just have to wonder what it's going to be like when we go back to our everyday life. Without June there...

I think we'll both miss her.

"How about you two make a whole lot of snowflakes and we can hang them up?" I suggest.

June gasps dramatically. "That's a great idea! What do you think, Pipes?"

She's even started using Piper's nickname. My heart couldn't grow any bigger.

"Then it'll be snowing inside!" Piper chirps.

"I'll take care of all the logistics. You two focus on the *art*," I say. Giving myself this project will be a good way for me to ignore all these feelings bubbling up about June.

June smiles at me and then holds up the scissors to Piper. "Come on! We have a lot of work to do."

While the girls work on the snowflakes, I make my way into the garage to grab the ladder. It's a rickety old thing I'm surprised hasn't rotted through, but it'll do the job. Then, I find some twine tucked in a drawer in the tool bench. This place is truly stocked as if there were people living here all the time. I think it'd be kind of nice to really get the hell out of dodge and live here where it's quiet, as opposed to the city. Even the suburbs are noisy and overcrowded.

I put the ladder in the middle of the living room, underneath the high beam rafters. Even on the top rung I'm going to be straining to get them hung up, but it's going to be worth it.

June and Piper come in with stacks and stacks of snowflakes. "We're ready, Daddy!" Piper announces.

"Great! Think fast!" I toss the ball of twine toward June.

June sticks out her hands, but the ball bounces between her hands until landing unceremoniously on the ground.

"Yeesh, not ready for pro ball, huh?"

June laughs. "I would have caught it if you hadn't taken me by surprise."

I try to school my face. My mind goes right back to our kiss. That certainly took us both by surprise. Luckily, June doesn't seem to notice what she's said. Maybe I'm making it a bigger deal than it was. One kiss between friends never hurt anyone. Except June isn't a *friend*. She's practically family in every way but blood.

I push down those thoughts and focus on helping the girls loop twine through slits in the paper snowflakes. They're all varying lengths to create the effect of snow coming down.

"Let's put them up!" Piper rushes over to the ladder and starts to climb, but I snatch her down before she can get more than a few rungs off the ground.

"Hold on, Pipes. This is a grown-up job. For me and June. Okay?"

Piper pouts. "Why? I want to climb the ladder."

"It's way too tall for you, honey. We gotta keep you safe," I say.

She starts to fuss; it's hard for me to stay calm when Piper's upset. I don't get mad, just stressed. Sometimes, I end up escalating the situation more than it needs to be. June, though, is pro at diffusing Piper's disappointment. "Listen, Piper, your daddy and I weren't able to climb ladders like this when we were your age. It's something you have to grow into."

Piper looks at June sadly. "Really?"

"I know it's hard to believe when Daddy is so tall!" June says with a smile. "But you'll be old enough and big enough in no time."

I hate to say it, but when June calls me "Daddy," it does things to me. It's so dirty, I know, but I can't help imagining her saying that to me in different, more intimate circumstances. Alone. With our clothes mostly off.

I need a cold shower.

"Piper, you can be the supervisor," June says. "You pick out the snowflakes and direct where you want them to go. Okay?"

Piper likes this idea. Any opportunity to be the boss. She picks out her first one and hands it to June. "Put it right there at the center."

"Okey dokey." June starts to climb the ladder.

I go to the ladder base and put my foot on the lowest rung to steady it. "You okay, June?"

"Oh yeah, I'm fine."

From this angle, I have a great view of her ass. Her little shorts leave little to the imagination. And, Jesus, I'd like to just take a bite out of it. I'm really not doing myself any favors if I'm supposed to work in the "forgetting about the kiss" department.

When she gets to the top, she has to balance on her tiptoes to get the twine around the support beam.

"Careful..." Piper says.

I'm bracing the bottom of the ladder as best I can. My mind, though, is playing out every worst case scenario. She falls and breaks her neck. She falls on Piper and breaks both their necks. She falls on me and we're both hurt leaving Piper alone without help. Dear god.

"There we go..." June pulls her hands back to reveal the snowflake. It hangs and wavers delicately.

Piper smiles brightly. "It's beautiful."

June starts back down the ladder slowly, but her foot catches on one of the low rungs. Her balance falters and she gasps. I'll be damned if anyone is going to get hurt on my watch. I launch myself up a few rungs and grab her bare thigh to steady her. "Whoa! Careful."

June clutches the rungs of the ladder. "Oh my god."

"You okay?" I ask. I haven't moved my hand. I'm afraid if I do, she'll fall.

She looks back at me, her enigmatic mismatched eyes wide. "Yeah, I think so."

I realize how tightly I'm gripping her thigh, my fingers creating deep imprints in her skin. I move my hand away as if her skin burns me and try to chuckle. "You scared me."

June tries to smile.

"You scared *me!*" Piper squeals. "I thought you were going to die!"

June makes it down the rest of the way, laughing. "Not today, Piper." When she's back on solid ground, she takes a deep breath. "Thank you."

My mouth is dry. "Don't mention it."

I can remember the feeling of her thigh. I clench my hand into a fist to get rid of it.

"Okay. Next one!" Piper holds up another snowflake.

June takes it. "Let's do it!"

Now I know not only the feeling of her lips, but of her body too. And both have intoxicated me.

I'm in trouble.

———

The rest of the morning is spent arranging the snowflakes around the living room. Once we're done, it's time for lunch. Afternoon is easy, breezy. I plop Piper down in front of the TV to watch some movies (hey, sometimes, a dad needs a break) while June does some job hunting. I, on the other hand, have to play some catch up.

I step into Dad's office, which he uses when he stays out here for extended periods, and give him a call from his big leather office chair. He picks up on the first ring. "Hey, Jare!"

"Hey, Dad."

"How are things out there?"

I already feel like I'm lying and I haven't said anything. "They're really good."

"Yeah? Did you guys get hit hard with the storm."

"Oh, yeah, it was rough. Things are finally starting to thaw and we got the driveway cleared, but I think we're going to finish up the week here."

"That sounds like a great idea. How's Pipes doing?"

I prop my feet up on the gargantuan oak desk. "She's doing great."

"Sunday dinner was so weird without you two. And June wasn't able to make it. Something with work, according to Keifer. So, it was just the three of us, Rye, and Rowan and Trev."

I make a sound of discomfort. "Yikes. How was that?"

"Awkward. Their rough patch only seems to be getting rougher."

I sigh. Trevor, Oliver's best friend, and his girlfriend, Rowan, have been an adorable couple for a little over a year. But after hitting that year mark, things have been tense between them. The honeymoon phase is wearing off. I know that feeling.

"Can I talk to Piper? I miss her like crazy."

"She's—uh—down for a nap right now. I can have her call you later," I say, although I don't know if that's a good idea. A three-year-old might not be the most skilled at discretion, and with how much fun she's having with June, I'm sure she'll spill the truth to her grandfather. "Anyway, I just wanted to check in and make sure that—"

"Everything is fine, Jarred. We miss you, but there's no

need to worry. The numbers will be here for you when you get back."

I smile. Good old numbers. Always accountable. "Sounds good."

"Give Piper a big hug and kiss from me, okay?"

"I will."

"Love you, kiddo."

"You too, Pops."

———

For dinner, June and I let Piper dictate the menu. She wanted mac and cheese, her favorite. Unsurprising. And June has an amazing recipe that uses all these different types of cheeses. She even sneaks cauliflower into the bechamel while Piper's back is turned, giving me a wink.

This is not going well. Instead of being able to forget about the kiss, everything is making me think about it more. Where does she get off winking at me like that? I don't even care that it's about sneaking vegetables into my daughter's food. It's making me feel things I shouldn't.

Piper is none the wiser about the cauliflower and devours two platefuls of the mac and cheese. "This is the best mac and cheese ever," she says with a mouthful.

"Piper, chew and swallow before talking," I admonish.

"It's good, isn't it? The kids I... the kids I used to work with love this recipe." June's smile falters as she says this. I bet she misses them.

"Piper's right," I say to her. "You're an amazing cook."

She blushes. "Oh, thank you. That's nice to hear. But it's just mac and cheese."

"Well, it's the best mac and cheese either of us ever had so that's not nothing," I say. "Seriously. It's awesome."

June pushes her fork around her plate. "I like doing it. So it's nice to hear that you like it."

My heart swells. Something about a woman wanting to take care of others does things to me. I'm not one to believe that women owe that to the world or that it's inherent to their nature. But to hear that it's something she enjoys doing... it makes me like her even more.

Fuuuuuck.

By the end of dinner, Piper's nearly falling asleep in her chair. Some days are just like that. "Okay, Pipes. Bath, and then bedtime."

"Noooo. I'm not tired," she replies through a yawn.

"Mmm, been there," June says with a laugh.

"Come on." I go to Piper and pick her up. "We'll read a few stories together. It'll be fun."

June starts to clear the table of plates. "I'll get things cleaned up down here."

"Would June tell me a story?" Piper asks.

I raise my eyebrows. "Um... no, Piper, June's cleaning down here and then–"

"June, would you tell me a bedtime story?" she asks before I can finish.

June stops midway between the sink and the kitchen table.

"You don't have to," I say. "I can–"

"No, no. I'd love that." June smiles. "You let Daddy get you all cleaned up, and I'll come read you a story, okay?"

Piper grins at me. "She said yes, Daddy!"

"I know she did. That means we have to be extra nice and clean and on our best behavior, hm?" I say before glancing at June. She's already at the sink washing the dishes, her back to me. Her beautiful auburn hair tumbles down her back and sways as she works. She's so used to caretaking. It comes naturally to her.

Man, I want a woman like her.

I take Piper upstairs and give her a bath. By the time she's all snuggled up under the covers, June waltzes in, ready for a bedtime story. "Are you all tucked in?"

Piper pulls her blanket up to her chin. "Goodnight, Daddy!" she announces and pokes her lips out for a kiss.

"Goodnight, Piper." I stroke her hair softly and give her a peck on the lips and then her forehead. Still my little baby. Always will be. "If you need anything, I'll just be... in the hall," I say to June as we exchange places.

"Thanks, Jarred," June replies and takes a seat beside Piper at the head of the bed.

No one else has had that spot except for me. It's strange to see June there next to my daughter like that. So close. So loving. I can't look away. I step into the hall but lean on the doorframe and watch as June begins to tell Piper a bedtime story.

"So, there was a little snow princess. And her name was–"

"Piper!"

"Oooh, that's a good name for a snow princess. And she was a very kind and smart princess. She ruled the Snow Kingdom with grace. And she had lots of animal friends like a snowy owl named–"

"Grandpa."

"*Grandpa* the snowy owl," June chuckles. "Alright. And a snow leopard named–"

"Uncle Oliver."

"And a majestic silvery horse named–"

"Victoria."

June laughs. "Victoria? Who is that?"

"It's a pretty name for a horse."

"Can't argue with that. Okay. Victoria."

Each moment I watch, my heart grows fuller. I don't even hear most of the story. I'm simply captivated by the image before me. My little girl feeling tenderness from someone who isn't me. The tenderness she deserves. It brings a tear to my eye. And to see how June adores her without ever pulling away makes me adore her even more.

Eventually, Piper falls asleep. June slips out from Piper's touch and turns out the bedside light before joining me in the hallway, shutting the door softly behind her. "How'd I do?" she whispers.

"G-great. You did. Yeah. Great." I'm stumbling over my words because I want to say so much more.

"Thanks for letting me do that. It's been hard, you know, with my job," June says, wrapping her arms around herself.

"Oh, she loved it. She loves you. Obviously."

June smiles up at me. I am getting that urge again in the pit of my stomach. She's so close. She's seems so willing. I want to kiss her.

I can't.

But I can keep her close.

"Do you want to have a glass of wine? Before bed?" I ask, gesturing to the staircase. "It's fine if not. I don't blame you if you just—"

"No, I'd like that."

I can't move. I'm trapped in her eyes.

"Cool."

"Cool."

I finally shake off my trance. "Uh. Red or white?"

"Whatever."

I start to back away. "Cool. I'll grab something from the cellar and meet you in the kitchen."

June smiles. "Sounds good."

The whole way down into the cellar, I feel like I'm walking on air. My heart pounds. It's clear to me I'm playing a dangerous game.

And I can't seem to stop.

11

———

JUNE

Jarred pours me a glass of wine, the red liquid sloshing like a storm on the ocean. "Thank you," I say in a voice smaller than I intend.

"You're welcome."

We're in the living room under the snowflakes hanging from the rafters. Every time I catch one out of the corner of my eye, I can't help but smile.

Jarred settles into a spot at the opposite end of the couch from me. We're almost far enough apart that it's awkward. Like, why are we sitting this far apart? It's making the elephant in the room even larger. The kiss has loomed in my brain since the second it happened. It put ideas into my brain I hadn't had before (or if I had, I was able to push them away).

Now, we're sharing a drink and don't know what to talk about. I sip my wine. "Mm. Good."

"It's fine," Jarred says with a twist in his lip.

I chuckle. "You Hawthorn guys and your wine."

Jarred blushes. "What's that mean?"

"Just... wine is wine to me. I can't taste if it's twelve dollars or twelve hundred dollars like you guys can."

He groans. "Man, it's embarrassing, isn't it?"

"No, it's charming. Just wish I could appreciate it the way you all do."

Jarred smiles softly into the bowl of his glass.

I sip some more wine, hoping I could understand what about it makes it "fine" versus "good," and I simply can't.

"She really likes you."

I look back at Jarred. His eyes are squared on me.

"Piper. She really, really likes you," he says and then looks away. "Always has, you know? But spending this time together... I can just tell she's very fond of you."

Through the veil of his blond, shoulder-length hair, I can see his brow is furrowed in contemplation. I know his mind is never far from Piper. That's the thing about being a parent. But he's had a rough go of it, having to take on being a single dad, especially when he's so young. He should be living up the last of his twenties like the bachelor he is. Dating and partying and doing whatever else it is bachelors do.

Instead, he's a dad. A good one. In the place of all that carefreeness is worry.

"I'm very fond of her too, Jarred."

That alleviates the tension on his face and he smiles again. "She has that effect on people."

"Yeah, she does. You're lucky. Not all kids are as good as she is."

"Trust me, I know. Although she's definitely a bit spoiled."

I laugh. "A bit? Have you seen your 'cabin in the woods'?"

"Okay, okay," he concedes. "A lot spoiled."

I knew the Hawthorns way before all of this. They didn't hit it big until we were nearly in middle school. I know they remember their life before all of that. But it's also impossible to not get caught up in wealth and all the privileges it brings. I understand. Even second hand, I get plenty of privilege, from gifts to trips to knowing I always have a safety net if I need one.

I mean, I'm here, aren't I?

I've drained my glass of wine faster than I intended. "Told you I liked it."

Jarred grins and pours me another glass. This time, he doesn't retreat to the total opposite side of the couch. He sits a little closer. I like it. "So, what made you come all the way out here?"

I frown. "What do you mean?"

"I mean, like, I know Keifer offered you the place. And you just lost your job. And you're renting your family house until the end of the month. But to come all the way out here instead of–"

"Instead of what?"

Jarred's eyes widen. "Sorry, I'm not trying to pry."

I swallow. "It's okay. I just don't know what you're asking."

"Don't you have somewhere to go in the city?"

I scoff. "Not really. I mean, I guess I could have stayed with Keifer, but you've seen his place. It's a pigsty."

"Right, no. He can't have women over there."

We both laugh. "That's really the only place I could go. You know?"

"You don't have other friends?"

"Well, sure. A handful. But they're all busy. I'd be a major inconvenience."

Jarred rolls his eyes. "You needed a place to go. That's not an inconvenience."

"Two weeks is a lot to ask of someone."

"Right, but that's what we do for each other. When we care about people, we go out of our way for them. And it all comes out in the wash, right? It balances out," he says, leaning an arm on the back of the couch, long legs drawn toward me.

I shake my head. "It's not that simple. I don't know. I don't like asking people for help because I feel like people always expect something in return. Or they use it against you." I've said too much. I take a big sip of wine. "I don't like to be a burden."

Jarred is quiet for a moment. "Well, you're not a burden to any of us, June."

That makes me happier than it should. I've been worried since he showed up here the other weekend that I've just been a thorn in his side. It's nice to know that he values me as a part of his family the way Keifer or his dad do. Although, if I'm a member of the family, I shouldn't be having dirty thoughts about him. Ever since he kissed me, my mind keeps rolling back to the feeling that parked between my thighs. Sure, it was just his lips on mine, but I felt it in my whole body. Now, every time he looks at me, touches me, says something to me, I can't help but remember the power he could have over me.

"Are you seeing anyone?" Jarred asks out of the blue.

I have my mouth on the lip of my glass when he asks. I snort into the wine and it bubbles inside the glass. "Sorry, that was gross." I wipe my mouth with the back of my hand. "Um. No."

"Was that a stupid question?"

"No. No, I'm just terminally single. It kind of comes

with the territory of nannying. Especially being a live-in. By the end of the day, I'm too exhausted to go out. Not to mention, where the hell would I bring someone if I wanted to... you know..."

Jarred gives me a lopsided smile. "Could make for some weird situations."

"Yeah, don't want a strange guy sneaking out in the middle of breakfast while the kids watch cartoons, you know?"

Jarred laughs. His cheeks are getting red from the wine. "I get it. I haven't managed a date in years."

"Years?"

"Yep. Well, actually, that's not totally true. I went on one," he says, topping off his glass with another splash of wine. "A little less than a year ago, I guess. And it was a blind date. A setup."

"Wow, like the olden days."

"Yeah, very much a pre-app vibe," Jarred replies. "Actually, it was one of Rowan's friends."

I widen my eyes. "Oh jeez."

"And somehow, she was actually crazier than Rowan."

"*Jarred*," I scold. "Rowan's not crazy."

"I mean it in a good way, of course!" Jarred says in defense. "She's wild. How about that?"

Wild is a good way to describe Rowan. She's likes to party hard and she's an adrenaline junky. But for all of her antics, she's smart as a whip and a whiz with computers. "Okay, so *wilder* than Rowan."

"Just way too impulsive for me. For an old fuddy-duddy dad. We went out to a nice dinner and midway through, she goes to the bathroom, and when she comes back... well, things just start getting weird. She's acting weird and her eyes are wide and then she says that I need to take her to the hospital."

"What?!"

"Turns out, she had taken shrooms before the date and the trip was going bad so when she went to the bathroom, she thought her face was melting off. She couldn't believe I couldn't tell," Jarred explains.

I stare at him in shock before bursting out into laughter. "You had to take her to the hospital because of a bad trip?"

"Yup."

"Oh, god, Jarred, I'm so sorry." I touch his shoulder sympathetically, unable to stop laughing.

"Yeah, needless to say, dating isn't my thing right now," Jarred says, running his fingers along the rim of his glass. "It's hard, especially since Piper is so young."

I realize that we've gotten closer over the past few minutes, the wine working like a magnet. I take my hand from his arm and tuck it under myself so I don't just pull him right into me. "One time, I went on a date with a guy and he left me in Kenosha."

"How did he leave you in Kenosha?"

"We thought it'd be fun to drive up to Kenosha just because, you know, why not?"

"How old were you?"

"Twenty."

"Aha..."

"Yeah... so we got up there and it was like midnight and we were starving. So, we stopped at a McDonald's and I ran inside to get us food. Well, between then and actually getting the order, he fell asleep and woke up and was so confused about where he was that he just drove off back home."

Jarred's turn to laugh. "What did you do?"

"Keifer ordered me an Uber. It was like two hundred dollars."

Jarred shakes his head. "What a jackass."

"It was an accident."

"Sure it was."

"It was! I swear. He was a nice guy, I don't think he was trying to be a jerk."

"No fucking way, you can't tell me that guy just forgot about the beautiful woman who had been in his car for two hours. That's ridiculous."

I suck on my lower lip. He just called me beautiful. And whether he meant to or not, I'm hanging onto it as if my life depends on it. "Yeah, I think he was just a dumb young guy. You know."

Jarred smiles and nods. "Oh yeah. I definitely know."

We are both quiet for a moment. Jarred resituates on the couch. His knee accidently brushes up against mine, but he doesn't draw away. "It doesn't make sense to me, though."

"That someone could forget a girl at a McDonald's?"

He shakes his head. "That someone as great as you doesn't have a bunch of guys chasing after her. You're like... totally perfect, June."

I freeze. Perfect? "You can't just say something like that."

Jarred frowns. "What?"

I put my glass of wine down and run my hands over my face. "You can't say I'm perfect or beautiful or anything like that."

"Why not?"

"Because!"

"Because why?"

In this short exchange, Jarred has shifted closer to me, so close I can smell the musk of red wine on his breath. Our eyes meet. God, he's so handsome. His dark eyebrows frame his eyes so perfectly; blue green, like diving into pristine, tropical waters. If I dive in, I won't want to leave. He hasn't shaved in a couple days; his stubble highlights how chiseled his jaw and cheekbones are. I want to touch his face so badly, kiss his plump lips.

"You know why," I whisper.

Jarred tilts his head to the side and then puts his wine glass next to mine on the table. "I didn't say anything but the truth. Surely there's nothing wrong with that?"

That does it. If he's going to sit there and say nice things about me, looking so fucking irresistible, I'm going to have to kiss him again. Doesn't matter that he's my best friend's older brother or that we're stuck in this cabin together. I have to.

I grab the inside of his knee and kiss him. I feel fireworks again through my whole body. This time, however, it's not sweet and chaste. It's hungry, as if we've been starving since the moment our lips parted last.

Jarred wraps his arms around me, pulling me into his lap so I'm straddling him. I thread my hands through the soft locks of his hair. Our chests are pressed together so tightly I can feel the wildness of his heart beating with mine. Without even thinking, I start to grind my hips against his. I can feel him growing right there between his legs. We've unleashed something, something bigger and untamed compared to our kiss yesterday morning.

I don't want to stop. Even though I know I should. I don't want to.

Jarred's hands slide around my hips, tightly locking me into place against his pelvis. He breaks away suddenly. "Goddammit, June."

"What?" I whisper, pressing a line of kisses up his neck to his jaw. His stubble pricks my lips.

"I've been trying so hard not to... but..." Jarred sighs in pleasure in response to my hips undulating against his. He slides his hands down my thighs and back to my waist. "...I want you so bad."

It's been a long time since I've heard a guy say something like that. A couple years. I've had my flings here and there, but they've been empty and lacking. Just sex for the sake of having it. This feels different. I cup his chin in my hand. "Your room or mine?"

Jarred's pupils dilate immensely at that suggestion. "You sure?"

I smile.

"I don't want to make you uncomfortable. I don't want to make this weird."

"I can already feel you getting hard, I think we're a little bit past the point of 'making it weird', Jare," I say and then kiss him softly. "Your room or mine?" I repeat.

Jarred half-laughs in disbelief. How did we get here? His guess is as good as mine. Perhaps it's been here all along. But I never saw it coming. Not in all my years of going to dinners at the Hawthorns. "Yours."

Jarred pushes us off the couch, picking me up in his arms as adeptly as he would Piper. I hook my legs over his hips and giggle as he walks us over to the stairs. "Jarred, stop, you'll drop me!"

"Only if you struggle!"

He starts up the stairs; it's not even cute anymore, I'm koala-ed onto him for dear life. "Jarred! Put me down!"

"I've got you!"

I grab onto the banister, desperate for anything steady.

Jarred jerks back and I slip out of his arms onto the stairs, making a thud as I land right on my ass.

"June!"

I burst into laughter. "I'm sorry! I got scared!"

Jarred joins me on the steps, trying to hold back his laughter. "Shh! Shh! You're being too loud, she'll wake up."

I cover my mouth to snuff out my laugh. I look over at Jarred. I still can't believe this is happening. Tripping over ourselves to get into bed together. This is the most fun I've had in months. I kiss him and then leap back to my feet. "Last one naked is a rotten egg!"

"Not fair! I wasn't ready!"

I sprint up the stairs and down the west wing hallway. Jarred is hot on my tail. I can hear his footsteps thumping behind me. It feels like we're kids, playing tag. I remember those first couple years after they moved into the mansion in Wilmette, the crazy games we'd get up to. We were just getting too old for them, but everything was so new and exciting, even Jarred who was definitely too old for games would get in on the fun.

Once I make it to my bedroom at the end of the hall, I throw off my T-shirt. I haven't been wearing bras while we've been laying around the cabin so I'm fully exposed. When Jarred bursts into the room, I turn around, arms wrapped around my chest, wearing a sheepish smile.

"Damn, you really want to jump right in, huh?" Jarred closes the space between us and touches my wrists. "Can I see?"

I let him untangle my arms away from my chest so my breasts are exposed. He inhales sharply. "Holy shit."

"Your turn."

Jarred smiles and obliges, pulling his sweatshirt up over his head, revealing his well-toned chest. "Not the same as when you do it," he murmurs and tosses the sweatshirt off to the side.

"No, it's fucking amazing," I say. I spread my palms over his pecs and admire the patch of chest hair originating from his sternum. "You're so sexy, Jarred."

"*You're* so sexy, June." He kisses me, putting his hands against my bare back and letting them fall lower and lower until they reach the waistband of my pants. "I don't even know how to act around you sometimes."

"Take them off," I say into his lips.

Jarred bites his lower lip, smiling. He pulls my pants down revealing me fully to him. He keeps going, pulling them all the way down to my ankles. "Step out."

I follow his instruction. "I'm sorry, I haven't shaved my legs in a while. You know, in the winter I just forget and–"

"I don't give a shit," he smiles. Jarred kisses the inside of my calf, then my knee, then my lower thigh, each kiss coming closer and closer to my lower lips. "I don't care at all."

I shiver when I feel his breath against my pussy.

"Smell so good, Juniper."

I don't know if I've ever heard him say my full name. Hell, I didn't even think he *knew* my full name. But the sound of it makes me melt.

"Can I taste?"

"Y-yeah."

Jarred pushes his face between my thighs and engulfs me in his mouth. I grab onto the bedpost for stability. Warmth spreads up from my pelvic bone to my stomach. Jarred's mouth feels like magic. My legs go weak. I fall back onto the edge of the bed. Jarred shoves me back further, not for a second breaking contact with my lower lips.

He ensnares my clit in his tongue. My body bends up in a shock of pleasure. "Fuck, that feels so good."

Jarred hums in satisfaction.

I grab the back of his head and pull him away from me. "Come here. Kiss me."

"I'm not done."

"Don't care."

Jarred comes up to meet my mouth; I taste my essence all over his lips and chin. I slide my hand down his chest to where his waist and hip create a V. His abdominals tense. He knows where I'm going. What I want. I keep going until my hand knocks up against the hot swell of his cock.

Jarred flinches.

I tug on the waistband of his pants. "Take these off."

He draws away, pulls down his pants and underwear, baring himself to me. Christ, he's big. Long and thick. I'm almost nervous to take it all, but I know the moment he enters me, I'll lose my mind. Jarred discards his clothes on the ground and looks at me. "We're naked, June."

I laugh. "Astute observation."

Jarred blushes. "I mean... you know what I mean, don't you?"

I do. There's so much history between us. We met when we were young enough to think the opposite sex had cooties and kissing was disgusting. Now, we're naked in bed together. About to do one of the only things Jarred and I probably shouldn't do together.

"You want to stop?" I ask. I don't want to stop, but I certainly don't want him to keep going just because of some impulsive consent.

A smile quirks onto Jarred's lips. "No."

"Good."

Jarred brings his body over mine and starts to kiss me

again. I feel his penis brush up against the inside of my thigh, drawing nearer to my already dripping center. The nervousness fades away almost instantaneously. Our tongues are dueling for dominance. I wrap my arms around Jarred to hold his chest to mine as if my life depends on it and wriggle my legs wider. I'm ready for him.

The head of his cock slides through my opening. We both laugh anxiously.

"You're so wet."

"Wonder whose fault that is?"

He chuckles and then adjusts his length, focusing on the space between us intently until the head finds my opening. He starts to push his hips forward. Taut muscles in my groin start to expand. I dip my head back and catch my breath.

"Am I hurting you?"

"No... just go slow."

Jarred thrusts shallowly inside me. Each stroke is like static electricity through my hips. Small and surprising. I push my face into his neck, breathing in his scent deeply. I want more of him. All of him that I can have. My hips start to commune with his.

"Deeper."

With each undulation, I pull him deeper into me. It feels so good to be full. I'm realizing I've felt so empty for so long. Not just literally, but in every part of my life. In just this week together, Jarred has made me feel so full.

"All of you. Give me all of you."

"Christ, June."

Jarred pushes his cock all the way to the hilt, his balls knocking up against me and I yelp in pleasure. "Fuck. Go faster."

Jarred grips the sheets on either side of me and starts to

thrust faster with his whole length. "Oh my god... you feel so good."

I don't have the ability to respond with words. All I can do is moan. He feels so good too. With each stroke, heat builds in the pit of my stomach. I can't remember the last time a man made me come, but I know it was nothing like this.

My legs start to shake. I'm losing control. Jarred feels so good and he's driving so deep inside me. I think I'm going to come sooner than I expected.

Jarred wraps his hand around my chin and jerks my face toward him. "Look at me."

I look into his eyes, gasping.

"Look at me when you come."

He can feel me clenching around him. He must know I'm close.

"Want to see how beautiful you look when I make you come."

Even in the throes of passion, he's sweet on me. "Jarred..."

"Yeah?" He revs his hips faster.

"Oh god, *Jarred.*"

"Let go, Juniper. Let go."

Just another pulse of his hips and the building electric coil inside me snaps. Heat blazes through my pelvis and up my body. I cry out, digging my nails into his back. He can't be close enough.

"I'm gonna come," Jarred grunts in my ear. "I'm gonna come, I'm..."

My pussy tightens around him. And then he releases. He whimpers in my ear, no longer in control. A total slave to his pleasure. I pull my face to his and kiss him as his orgasm crests, our teeth knocking together from need.

We're both sweaty and breathing heavily, basking in the glow of making each other feel fucking amazing. "How did you do that?" I ask. "Make me feel like that?"

Jarred laughs and falls into the pillow next to me. "I only wanted to make you feel good."

"Well, it worked."

"Yeah?"

"Yeah."

He kisses me softly. "You made me feel good too." Jarred pushes some hair back out of my face. "You *make* me feel good, June."

Jarred's still inside me. Somehow, he hasn't deflated. I can still feel his virility pulsing. There's more work to be done. More pleasure to be had. I lock my eyes in his. Blue green. Ocean. I'm diving in.

"Do it again," I say raggedly.

Jarred understands. He slowly drags one of his hands down to my bare breast and pushes his thumb against my nipple. I jerk under him. "As many times as you like, Juniper."

12

___

JARRED

I wake up burrowed under the covers, warm and cozy as can be. God. My dreams were crazy last night. No more wine before bed. I'm getting to that age I guess.

It's going to be hard to face June today after having dreams all night long about being with her. Like that. They felt so real and just went on and on and on.

I open my eyes sluggishly, adjusting to the gray morning light. Wait a second. The wall seems closer than it usually does. Is my room really this small? I rub my eyes and try to refocus.

Suddenly, the bed shifts. Something moves. I sit up in terror and find that, next to me, is the woman from my dream.

June.

What the fuck? That was *real*?

I stare at her for a moment. She's facing away from me, her dark hair splayed across her pillow. My eyes travel down to her neck to her upper back. She's not wearing a shirt.

Oh my god.

I lift the sheets. Fuck, I'm buck naked.

June shifts again, this time turning on to her back and stretching her arms up. "Mm. You awake?"

"Um. Yeah."

June's eyes squint open and she smiles. "Good morning."

I stare at her wide-eyed. "Morning."

She laughs groggily. "You okay?"

Her morning voice is sexy, laden with sleep and dreaminess. "Uh. Yeah. Listen, did we... last night?"

June raises an eyebrow. "You don't get that drunk off two glasses of wine, do you?"

"N-no. I just–" I stop short and purse my lips.

She pushes herself up onto her elbow. The blanket falls away slightly to reveal her bare chest, but only for a moment. She yanks the blanket back over her chest. "Are you upset?"

"God, no," I say with a breathless laugh. "No. It was great. For me. Was it... was it good for you?"

June smiles and nods. "Yeah. Really good."

That's nice to hear. "I just can't believe it happened."

"Yeah... kind of crazy."

We are both quiet for a moment.

"We don't have to talk about it," June says. "We can just pretend it never happened."

I frown. "Is that what you want?"

"Isn't that what *you* want?"

God, I hate this game of chicken that always happens after spending a night with someone. The trying to read if we had a nice time rather than just being totally honest. I'm too old and been through too much to play these games. "Listen, June. In the real world, this..." I gesture between the two of us. "Can't happen."

She nods. We don't need to go through all the details. We're basically family. It'd be wrong.

"But here is kind of like not the real world. And if you'd be cool with it, I wouldn't mind continuing to–well, you know..." As soon as it comes out of my mouth, I feel like I sound like an asshole. A sex-driven, emotionless shell of a guy. One of those fucker frat boys in River North always on the hunt for a new girl to bang.

June's smile, though, alleviates my fears of sounding like an asshole. "What happens at the cabin, stays at the cabin."

"Right! Exactly. Totally. Because last night was really nice."

"*Really* nice."

I grin. "I'm glad you agree."

"Shake on it?" June holds out her hand to me.

I take it and immediately feel all the emotions from last night come back. The way her arms felt around me, the way her lips felt on mine, the feeling of being inside her. Juniper Reed is doing something to me.

And as much as I shouldn't, I like it. In fact, I love it.

"Gotcha," June says with a sneaky smile and pulls me into her. Our lips find one another's with ease, as if we've known our bodies a lot longer than just one night. I relax again into her bed. The warmth and closeness of her is stirring. I already feel myself getting hard.

"Shit, Piper!" I exclaim, pulling back. "I left her in the east wing alone all night. What if something–"

"Nothing happened, Jarred," June says in a voice as smooth as satin. "I promise. She's okay. Just be here with me a little longer."

I can't say no to her. This is bad. We kiss for a while, wetly and sloppily. Our bodies fit into one another's so perfectly. I know all her hills and valleys like the back of my hand. I already have favorite parts of her. Her ass, plump and juicy in my hand, the hollow of her clavicle, the mole on her ear.

If I can only have June for a few more days, I want to make the most of it.

June's hand finds my cock; I gasp, pushing my hips into her hand. "You've got such a nice dick, Jarred."

I swoon. It might seem stereotypical, but hearing a beautiful woman compliment my manhood is an aphrodisiac like no other.

She starts to slide her hand up and down. "Felt so good inside me."

"Shit, June..."

"Wonder what you taste like."

"Oh my god," I whine.

June darts below the covers and slips my penis into her mouth without another word. Euphoria emanates through my pelvis. Hidden below the covers, she moves up and down in a perfect rhythm. I watch with my jaw fallen open. One of her hands clings to my thigh and the other works in tandem with her mouth, stroking my shaft up and down.

"Jesus, June, your mouth...."

Who knew that little June Reed had this in her? I sure didn't. And no Hawthorn man ever should. But I get to. I feel so lucky.

The sounds of her taking my cock into her mouth are divine. Slurping and sucking with all her might. All of a sudden, June grips my hips and slides my whole cock into her mouth. My whole body jumps. "Holy shit. Holy *shit*."

Even the sound of her gagging is beautiful.

I lift the blankets so I can watch her. Her eyes immediately flick up to mine. One hazel, one dark as night. I feel like I've been cornered by a mythic temptress. She's trapped me under her spell. But can I be trapped when I have so willingly given into her?

These next few days are going to be fucking incredible.

Her mouth curls into a smile. She takes one hand and starts to massage my balls. I feel them tightening, ready to release into her mouth. But suddenly, she slides me out of her mouth. I bristle at the cold. "Say my name, Jarred."

"June..."

She shakes her head. "My full name."

I give her a tired smile. "Juniper."

June bats her eyes coquettishly and puts the head of my cock back in her mouth.

"You like that? You like that, *Juniper?*"

June moans around my length. I start to tremble.

"Your mouth feels perfect, Juniper. I'm so close."

She goes back to her rhythm, faster this time. Warm, tickling pleasure is ready to seep into every nerve of my body.

"Fuck. Juniper."

Faster.

"How are you doing that? How are you going so–" The head of my cock hits the back of her throat and I let out a curdling moan.

June digs her fingers into my thighs and keeps working at her breakneck pace.

I'm going to come. I have to come.

"I'm gonna–can I? Can I come?"

"Mhm..." she hums.

"Can I–oh, god, I'm–I'm–" My balls tighten a bit more and then I fall over the edge of release. My cock spasms in her mouth. "I'm coming. Shit, I'm coming in your mouth."

June moans around me, sucking up every last drop. Gladly.

I wrap my hand around the back of her head and hold her there, jerking my hips into her mouth to release every last bit. It feels so good. Like I'm in free fall and I'll never hit the ground. As soon as she's sucked me dry, I collapse into the pillows. June releases me tenderly, laying my shrinking cock against my stomach. She wipes the corners of her mouth and smiles at me. Proud.

"What the fuck was that?"

"Some would call it a blowjob."

I laugh, shaking my head, and pull her up against my chest. It may be freezing outside, but here with June, I'm warm as can be. Her naked body on mine is all the heat I need. "You're fucking amazing, June." Then, I tuck my mouth up against her ear. "Juniper."

Her body breaks out in goosebumps. It's that easy, hm? I'll keep that in mind.

"I'm glad you liked it," she whispers.

I kiss her on the lips I can faintly taste myself. How'd I get so lucky? To get trapped with someone who's not only amazing in bed, but also hilarious and great with my daughter?

"Okay. Now, I really need to go check on Piper," I say, although all I really want is to be stuck here under June. Beautiful June. She really is like June. Like a lilac tree or the longest day of the year. Her sun has lit up my life in a way I didn't know Piper and I needed.

"I'll go get started on breakfast," June says softly.

"No, no. You rest. You fucking deserve it after that."

June laughs and I kiss the side of her head. "Fine. I won't argue with that."

I release her and slink out of bed, as much as I don't want to, and start to put my clothes back on. "You know, we have to keep it cool around Piper."

"Of course."

"I'd hate to make her think we're something that we're not."

"I wouldn't dream of it, Jarred," June replies emphatically.

I pull my shirt back over my head and look at her. She's tucked back under the covers, nude shoulders peeking out. "But later tonight..."

June grins. "You've got ideas?"

"For you, Juniper, I have millions of ideas," I say. I haven't been this smooth in years. I guess it's easy with the right person.

"I'll be looking forward to it."

I back out of the room, wanting to savor this image of June. I'll need it for the rest of the day. One final look, and then, I open the door and sneak back into the hallway. I come face to face with the mounted deer head and almost yelp in fright. It's big, black eyes are staring into my soul as if it knows all my secrets.

"Don't look at me like that," I mumble.

Back in the hallways of the cabin, I remember the stakes of this. My family. Keifer. What June and I are doing has to remain a secret for all eternity if we don't want to hurt anyone. I think we can make it happen as long as we're careful.

I go to the east wing and quietly open Piper's door. She's still curled up in bed, none the wiser to the fact I wasn't sleeping right next door. I go sit on the edge of the bed and tenderly stroke her cheek. My little baby girl. "Good morning, Piper."

Piper stirs. She grabs my wrist with her little hand. "Mmgh."

"Time to get up."

She opens her eyes. A big smile spreads onto her lips. "Daddy, I had a good dream last night."

"Hm? What was it?"

"Me and you went on a trip. And June was there. And we did all sorts of fun things. But we all learned to fly. And then June was like my mommy because I kept calling her 'Mommy.' And we all had a nice time."

My insides wrench together. It's just a dream, but dreams say so much about our realities. Piper and June are getting close. Too close, maybe. "That sounds like a good dream, baby."

"Did you have any dreams last night, Daddy?"

"Hmm... yeah. Some good ones. I can't remember what happened, though."

Piper laughs. "That's silly."

"I know. But I'm old and forgetful."

She shakes her head and wraps her arms around my neck. I melt into her hug with everything I have. I would give this girl the world. The whole fucking world, if I could. But the one thing I can't give her is a mother. At least not without the help of another person. And I don't know if I have it in me to trust someone like that. Piper and I have already been scarred. I couldn't do that to her again.

"Come on. Let's go make some breakfast."

We head downstairs, but by the time we hit the last step, I can already hear June clanging away in the kitchen. Such a busybody. I smile to myself.

Piper wiggles out of my arms and bounds into the kitchen. I follow her and get to watch her excitement as she sees June. "Good morning, June!"

"Piper! Good morning!" June exclaims and opens her arms wide. Piper leaps into them and gives her a big hug. "What do you say to pizza for breakfast?"

"Pizza? For breakfast?!"

"Yes! Pizza for breakfast!" June replies. She looks fresh and clean; how she did that in just fifteen minutes, I'm not sure. "What do you think?"

Piper looks back at me. "I've never had pizza for breakfast. What do you think, Daddy?"

I smile. They look perfect together, totally adore one another. June will be a great mom someday. It's obvious. A part of me could picture her and Piper together, bonded intimately like mother and daughter. But we've made a deal. All we are to each other is lovers, and just for the next few days. Something inside me tightens, but I can't focus on it right now.

"There's a first time for everything, Pipes."

Piper squeals in excitement. "Okay! Pizza for breakfast! How do we start?"

"Let me show you," June says and begins to explain the meal to Piper.

No, I can't focus on how it makes me feel when I watch them together. Once we're back in Chicago, it's back to me and Piper against the world.

13

—————

JUNE

The next few days blend together in the best way possible. Everything feels good and easy. During the day, Jarred and I have fun with Piper. At night, we have fun with each other. It's the best of both worlds. I've done every winter activity I can think of and then some, some I hadn't done since I was a little girl.

Hawthorn's Haven really *is* a haven. Away from the city, from the drama. It exists as its own little bubble. Which makes what's happening between Jarred and me even easier to plan on letting go.

Don't get me wrong, I like Jarred. In another world where we weren't practically family, maybe we would find our way to one another. We have similar senses of humor and aren't afraid to get too silly, especially when it comes to Piper. We're both compassionate and caring. And the chemistry we have is truly out of this world.

Jarred and I have fucked in positions I didn't even realize *were* positions. I haven't gotten more than five hours of sleep in a single night because Jarred and I are keeping each other up. Most of the time, it's from the sex, but sometimes, it's the pillow talk afterward.

"Pipes and I are going to leave Saturday morning," Jarred croaks. I'm tucked into his arms after he's just made me come three times in one session. The man has skill and I am worried no other man will ever compare.

It's Thursday night. One more day before they leave. "Wish this didn't have to end," I say into his neck.

"Mm. I know. It's so nice to be away from everything. And to not work," Jarred replies.

"Definitely. As soon as we're back in Chicago, it's back to the grind. Or lack thereof, I guess."

Jarred squeezes me. "You'll find something, June."

"Hope so." I've sent in my resume to several potential families, but without the reference from my most recent family, people must be skeptical of how that all shook out. I haven't gotten even a nibble from a potential employer.

"I can pass your resume around Piper's pre-school. And I can tell you the families to stay away from."

"Oooh... the inside scoop."

"Precisely."

I nuzzle my face into his chest. "That'd be nice, Jarred. Thank you."

He rubs his hand up and down my back. I could fall asleep right here in his arms, and I have. I feel so safe with him. Perhaps it's the history we have together. And sure, that's the thing that's keeping us apart, but it's also the thing that's kept us near to one another all these years. I like feeling safe and small in his arms. I haven't felt safe and small in years. Not even with my own parents.

"How about tomorrow we take Piper sledding?"

"That's a great idea," I say.

"It's a short hike to the sledding hill. It's going to warm

up tomorrow and most of the snow will be melted by the end of the day, but if we go bright and early, we'll have a great time, I think."

"Piper will love that."

Jarred looks at me. He quietly regards my face, eyes scanning me.

"What?"

He shakes his head. "Just so pretty."

I blush. "I'm going to miss you calling me pretty."

Jarred kisses the side of my head. "Don't act like we're already saying goodbye, June. We've still got a day."

Yes, we still have a day. But honestly, I don't want to say goodbye. I think that might just break my heart.

I can't believe I'm admitting it, but I'm falling for Jarred. And if he asked, I'd make it work with him. We'd find a way to tell Keifer. He is a grown man, perfectly capable of dealing with it. He is my best friend and he'd want me and his brother to be happy, right? And I'd take on motherhood in a heartbeat. I'd bend my whole life to fit around him.

I want him.

I close my eyes and rest my head on his chest. I can hear the thumping of his heart. It lulls me to sleep, almost as if it's whispering, "Keep me... keep me... keep me..." And I wish I could. I really want to.

I'm a grown-up, though. I can't have everything I want. So I have to make this last day count.

———

"You didn't say this hill was so big, Jarred." We're standing at the top of the sledding hill we talked about in bed last night. And, man, it's a doozy.

"You're just used to having to find sledding hills in

Chicago which don't even count," Jarred scoffs. "Right, Piper?"

"Right!"

I have to laugh. Piper is decked out like she's about to go on a mission across the arctic tundra. A full body snowsuit, ski goggles, a scarf that can wrap around her about three times. "Well, someone's ready to sled, huh?"

"You bet. Come on, Pipes. We'll go together." Jarred puts the two person sled down and sits at the back. He pats the place in front of him. "A perfect, Piper-sized spot right here."

Piper wedges herself between his legs and grabs his shins. "I'm ready."

"Give us a push, will you, June?"

"Okay, but don't say I didn't warn you..." I grab the back of the sled and start to push it forward. "See ya!" I cry out as the sled tips over the edge of the hill.

It swoops down. Jarred and Piper hoot and holler on the way down, the sled picking up speed until the ground evens out again. "How was it?" I call out.

"Amazing!" Piper yelps. "Again! I want to go again!"

The walk up is nearly four times the length of the ride down, especially through the remains of the snow. Jarred hoists the sled up on his back. "Okay, June, your turn."

"Me? No. This is for you guys. I'm just a spectator," I say.

"What, are you scared?" Jarred teases me, a smirk on his lips.

I can't resist that look. I've seen it so many times in bed. When he looks up at me from between my legs, knowing how he's pleased me with his tongue or when we're in the midst of foreplay. "N-no, I'm not scared."

"Come on, June! Don't be chicken!" Piper says, grabbing onto my leg and shaking me.

"I'm not a chicken!"

"June's a chicken!" Jarred teases and then makes a clucking sound that's stunningly accurate.

"Bock bock! June's a chicken!" Piper imitates as best she can. She's reeling with laughter.

I roll my eyes. "Fine! If it makes you happy. I'll go down. But Daddy has to go down with us too."

Jarred raises an eyebrow. "Well, it's a two person sled, June."

"We're friends here, right? We can all squeeze."

Jarred's wind-brushed cheeks grow even redder.

"That'll be fun! Let's all go!" Piper announces. "Daddy, you have to get on first, because you're the biggest."

"Yeah, Daddy, you have to get on first," I echo.

Jarred gives me a warning look. I can see his pupils dilate briefly. I wonder how he'll get back at me later. "Fine. Here." Jarred sits as far back on the sled as he can. "June?"

He holds out a hand for me and guides me into my spot in front of him.

"You have to get closer if we're all going to fit," he murmurs.

I back up so I'm right in between his legs, my ass flush to his pelvis. If we weren't wearing so much winter gear, I bet I could feel him hardening. "Is this close enough?"

Jarred smiles. "Perfect."

"Okay, Piper! You now!" I announce.

Piper finds her spot again, nestled between my legs. "See? We all fit. Three peas in a pod!"

"Something like that," Jarred mutters. "Okay, now we all have to pull the sled forward. You ready?"

We all work as hard as we can to pull the sled forward,

grabbing onto the ground and shifting our hips back and forth. It's a laughable effort, but we finally make it to the tipping point.

"Everyone hold on!" Jarred announces.

My heart is beating fast. I grab onto the edges of the sled as tight as I can. "Oh god."

"Here... we... go!"

My stomach flips as gravity takes control. The sled starts to slide down the hill and picks up speed alarmingly quickly. "Oh my god, oh my god, oh my god!" I repeat over and over. "Piper, hold on!"

"We're going so fast!" she screams joyfully.

But I can tell we're going *too* fast. The added weight has got us speed off past their stopping point and toward a big, wide oak. I wrap my arms around Piper, ready to pull her out of harm's way, when Jarred sticks his foot out; the sled spins out away from the tree at just the last second, but the power of his braking sends us all flying into the snow.

The coldness whips against my face. I lay there breathing heavy for a few moments. "You guys okay?"

"Yeah, I think so." Jarred's close by. "Piper?"

"That was *amazing*!" Piper screams. I hear her boots crunching toward me. "Did you see? We almost crashed!"

I turn onto my back and look up at the sky. It's soon eclipsed by Piper's smiling face. "Let's do it again!"

Jarred has already gotten to his feet. He swipes her up into his arms. "No, no. I think we'll stick to just two riders from now on. Why don't you grab the sled and start up the hill, okay?"

Piper follows his instructions. Then, Jarred holds his hand out to me. "You're not hurt, are you?"

"No, just in shock, I think," I say through a laugh. I take his hand and let him pull me up to my feet.

We are standing face to face, only a couple inches apart.

"Thanks," I say softly.

Jarred looks askance to Piper who is incredibly focused on climbing. He leans in toward me and kisses my cheek. My whole body, which had been laden down with the cold, now feels as warm as a fire. "How does it feel to not be a chicken?" he asks in a low voice.

I laugh and push him playfully on the chest, before starting to make the walk up the hill. "You're an ass."

Jarred follows. "No, you *like* my ass. There's a difference."

I gape at him. "*Jarred!*"

"You do! You told me last night."

"Your daughter is *right there.*"

"You said, 'Oh, Jarred, let me get a piece of that cake.'"

I laugh loudly. "I did *not* say that!"

"You're taking forever!" Piper screams from the top of the hill, arms crossed over her chest.

Jarred and I immediately stop our flirtation and exchange a sheepish glance. We'll have to save it for later. And I have no doubt we both will have a lot in store for each other.

14

JARRED

Nighttime. Late. June and I have snuck into the master bath and run the water so hot it's steaming. It's full to the brim with bubbles. We sit on opposite sides, sipping champagne garnished with strawberries, our legs entangled under the water.

"This feels perfect," I murmur, leaning my head back and closing my eyes.

"I know. After the day we've had..."

We were so tired from sledding, I was almost worried we weren't going to find the energy to be intimate at all. But the second June suggested we take a bath together, I knew that would change. She's always full of ideas. Life is certainly never boring with her around. I'll miss that when we leave tomorrow.

"Hey."

I lift my head and peek an eye open. "Hm?"

June holds her glass out toward me. "A toast."

I hold my glass out to meet hers. "To?"

"To Hawthorn's Haven."

"I can't argue with that."

Our glasses clink together and we both sip our champagne. June puts her glass to the side and picks up a strawberry. Her dark hair is piled up on top of her head. She looks like a siren or a mermaid. "So. What are you going to tell everyone about your little getaway?"

I watch her lips engulf the strawberry sensually. Can't help but think about how her mouth looks around my cock. "Um. That it was a nice time."

"How are you going to keep Piper quiet?" she asks.

"Bribery, probably."

June laughs. Her laugh is like the clouds parting for the sunshine.

"Don't judge me. If I can keep her quiet about all this with a couple toys and maybe tickets to Disney on Ice, it'll all be worth it."

"Hey, I'm not judging. I've done plenty of bribery in my day while working with kids. It's part of the game."

I smile. She really gets it. "Give me one of those, would you?"

June takes a strawberry and wades through the water toward me so she's situated in my lap. "Open up."

I open my mouth and let her put the strawberry between my lips. I bite down, the juice running down my chin. Tastes good. But not as good as her.

June licks the juice of my chin and then kisses me softly.

"You're pretty," I say.

"Yeah?"

"Yeah."

"You're not just saying it because you know I like to hear it?"

I shake my head. "No. You're very pretty. Some guy is going to be really, really lucky one day."

Her expression falters and her eyes drop from mine.

"Well, if you have any friends to set me up with, I'm available."

"I don't think any of my friends are as good in bed as me, unfortunately."

June snickers. "Is that from firsthand experience?"

"No."

"Because I'd be happy to put that theory to the test."

She starts to move back to her side of the tub, but I wrap my arms around her and hold her to me. "Now, wait a second..."

"Hm?"

"I'm not done with you yet. You can't be talking about fucking all my friends."

"You're not done with me, hm?"

I run my hands down her slick body. The curves I've come to learn and love so well in these few short days. "No. Not done by a longshot."

"Am I in for a long night?"

"Very long."

"I don't know how you have the energy to go so many times. I've never met a man with such a short recovering period."

I guide her hips up and position her over my lap. The bubbles create a veil over her tits, but I can see her ruby nipples poking through. "It's all you, June. You do that to me."

June bites her lower lip.

"Fuck, you're so sexy."

She pushes her fingers through my hair, sending chills down my spine. "You like that?"

"Feels nice."

She scratches my head softly. "When did you realize I was so sexy, Jarred?"

"Huh?"

"Did you just have a wakeup call the past few days?"

"Honestly? Yeah… kind of."

June takes her hands away from my head. "Wow. Thanks."

"No, no, listen, hey." I rub her back lovingly. "You've always been off-limits. I've never thought you were ugly or unattractive. I just had you in a box of people that aren't available to me my whole life. You know?"

June eyes me suspiciously.

"Haven't I been in your off-limits box?"

She rolls her eyes upward, thinking. "Yes. I suppose."

"Right. So when you were here and I didn't expect it, you took me off-guard. And somehow, you got out of that box."

"I see."

"Now, I can't unsee it. You're gorgeous, June. And just…" I take a deep breath. I shouldn't say it. But I'm too tired and the champagne is too bubbly. "You're amazing."

June's face softens. She takes a deep, heartened breath. "You're amazing too."

We can't sit in this. If we do, we're both doomed. "Sorry to ruin the moment, but I'm so hard right now, I–"

"Oh, I know. I can feel it."

"You're ruthless, June. Juniper."

June touches my hard cock under the water and adjusts it under her. "I'm going to ride you."

"Go for it."

She sinks down onto my cock, letting out a long, nearly pained breath. "Shit, you feel so good, Jare."

The water adds a whole other element to the stimulus of sex. We can't get too wild if we don't want to make a mess. But the warmth heightens every feeling inside. As

June starts to raise and lower herself, I already feel so good.

June puts her hand against my chest. "Relax."

I lean back against the tub.

"Let me take care of you."

I rest my hands on her hips, but let her take control. June rides with grace and elegance. Up and down, her head rolling around as feeling flows through her. Her breasts bounce with her pulsing hips. It's hypnotic. I grab each one in my hands and roll her nipples between my fingers. June's body jerks; she gasps, "Oh, yes, keep doing that."

I'll do whatever pleases her. That's how far gone I am. "You like it when I touch your tits?"

"Nngh. Yeah."

"You like it when I–" I tweak her nipples again.

"Oh, fuck, yeah."

Her hips are moving faster. The water sloshes. I can feel myself building to a climax, but my attention is on June. I want her to come first, always want her to come first. I continue to play with her nipples, following the lead of her hips. "Good girl. Keep going. Ride me."

June grabs onto the edge of the tub, leaning over me. "I'm close."

"Keep going. Use me, baby."

I slide in and out of her, faster and faster. I burrow my face in her neck and nibble on the sensitive skin. June mewls in response. "Yes. That. Yes, Jarred."

Between having her on my cock, rolling her nipples, and working her neck with my mouth, I know she's close. But she's getting tired and slowing down.

"Close, baby?"

"Yeah."

I grab her hips and hold them tight to mine while I drive

into her like a jackhammer. The water splashes; June's voice echoes off the bathroom walls as she whimpers and moans. "Oh my god, oh my god, oh my..."

"Yes, baby. That's it. Come for me."

June climaxes. Her eyes roll back and her whole body spasms. "Fuck. *Fuck.*"

I hold onto her, keep her safe, but my own orgasm rolls through me. My hips jump up as I empty inside her without warning. "I got you. I got you, baby."

June falls limply over my shoulder. Her fingers play with my hair. "Mm. Thank you. That felt so good. Thank you, Jarred."

I almost say "any time," but that wouldn't be true. It won't be any time. This might be the last time we fuck if we don't make time in the morning before Piper wakes up. Instead, I don't say anything. I embrace her tightly and nestle into her neck.

"How are you going to put me back in your box, Jarred?"

"My 'do not touch' box?" I chuckle.

"Yeah. Because I don't know how I'll put you in mine."

My stomach drops. That's a scary thing to hear. Have we taken this too far? Will June be able to let me go?

I shake off the feeling. Of course she will. We both have to. For Keifer. That's her best friend, my brother. We'll make sacrifices for him. "I think I'll put you in a new box."

"What box is that?"

"Things I'm glad I've touched and will never get to again."

15

———

JUNE

"You're all dug out now, right?" Keifer asks.

His voice has never been so unwelcomed. I've talked to him mostly through text or Instagram chats the past week and half. Every time he's called, I've ignored him. I know he's going to start being suspicious if I keep sending him to voicemail. "Yep. I am."

"Great. So you won't have a problem getting out on— when are you coming back?"

"Tuesday," I say, sucking on my lower lip.

"Tuesday. Great. I'm free that night. I'll come over to the house and bring dinner."

"Sounds good."

Jarred sneaks past me carrying a bag. He gingerly places it by the front door on the stack that's already there. He tiptoes dramatically past me and I have to hold in a laugh.

This morning, I woke up to him hard at my back. We had slow, drawn out morning sex. It was a goodbye, although neither of us said that. Neither of us said much, in fact. It was all implied.

I didn't enjoy myself quite as much as I have every other time we had sex. I have to say it. I'm sad to see them go and to say goodbye to the haven we've created. I have a couple more days here until the month is up and then I can finally go back home.

I stare at the bags sitting by the front door. I wouldn't mind staying here longer, though. Maybe even forever.

"June?"

I look down at Piper who has sidled up beside me while I've been zoned out.

"What was that?" Keifer asks.

"Huh?"

"That noise?"

I hold my finger out to Piper for her to give me a second. "Oh, just a creaky door hinge. You know how this place is?"

Keifer laughs. "Do I ever. It really needs an update."

"I like it just fine. Hey. Listen. I have to go. I left some water boiling on the stove top. I'll call you back when I'm finished." I don't even wait for him to reply, just hang up on him. "Sorry, Piper. What is it, honey?"

"Why won't you come with us?"

"Oh, Piper, I'm coming back to Chicago in just a couple days. I won't be stuck here forever," I say with a smile.

She looks away shyly, folding her hands together in front of her dress. "But why won't you come with me and Daddy?"

I bite my lower lip. I knew this would be difficult. I crouch down and take her hands in mine. "Well, honey, you know, Daddy and I have been friends for many, many years. And because of that, you and I have been friends for a long time too. So, we will always be friends. But friends don't live together, at least not usually. You know what I mean?"

Piper still is hiding her face from me.

"Honey?"

A few tears fall from her cheeks. "I want you to come with us."

"I know how you feel, Piper. But I can't."

She sniffles. I want to pull her into my arms and hold her, but then I'm afraid I'd never let her go. How did this all become so complicated so fast?

"What's going on?" Jarred asks, walking into the front hallway.

I look at him; he looks amazing in a white dress shirt and tie. He's dressed for his old life. It's clear he's ready to leave this all behind. Leave *us* behind. I'm mad at how much that's hurting my heart.

"I don't want to leave June!" Piper cries out, tears streaming down her face.

"Oh, no. Okay. Come here, baby." Jarred takes Piper up in his arms and rocks her side to side. "We'll see June soon. Next weekend."

Piper buries her head in his shoulder. "But I don't want to wait."

"I know, honey." He rubs her back, letting her cry. His eyes flick to me briefly. I try to smile.

"I love June, Daddy."

Jarred takes a deep breath. "I know you do."

"I love you too, Piper," I say. I'm not sure it'll help but I have to try. "This isn't goodbye forever. Just a see you later."

Piper lifts her head and wipes her eyes to look at me. "Okay."

"And you can always remember all the fun things we did. And the snowflakes. We have so many new memories together. Isn't that special?" I ask. My heart is breaking. I'm thinking about Harvey and Ellen too, the children I left behind that I didn't get to say goodbye to. I wonder if they were in the same kind of pain Piper's in.

Piper reaches for my hand and I take it. The three of us are so close in this moment. We're almost like a little family. I kiss her hand. "It's time to say goodbye, honey."

That doesn't help at all. She just starts to cry again.

"Oops. Sorry."

"It's okay," Jarred sighs. "Let me take her out to the car and then I'll come grab the rest of the bags, okay?"

I nod. "Okay."

I stand in the front hallway and wait for him. What will our goodbye be like? How will it feel? I'm scared. What if I burst into tears just like Piper? As soon as they leave, I'll be alone again. I don't know if I want to go back to that sadness.

Jarred opens the front door and slips inside. "Left the car running for her. So I have a minute."

I smile sadly. "Okay."

He comes over to me; we look at each other. The house is so quiet.

"Drive safe," I say.

"Thanks. You too."

"This was fun."

"Yeah. It was." Jarred puts his hands in his pockets. It's clear he doesn't know what to do just as much as I don't. Fuck this is a mess. "Thanks for all your help with Piper."

"I'm sorry she's so upset."

"It's okay. She'll get over it."

That breaks my heart a little. She'll get over me. Just like he will. And once again, I have to wonder who do I matter to?

"Can I kiss you?" Jarred asks. "One more for the road?"

I smile. "Yeah. Please."

Jarred leans in and kisses me on the lips. It is a tender kiss. Not the ones we've been hiding in the folds of the night with our bodies intertwined. Softer. More careful. I reach for one of his hands and squeeze it. My eyes are filling with tears. Maybe I should say something. But what the hell would I say? Don't go? Stay? Take me with you?

I want to be with you?

It would never work. We said it from the beginning. What happens at Hawthorn's Haven, stays at Hawthorn's Haven. There's no letting it go beyond these walls. Just like Piper's memories of this time will have to be enough, so will mine.

But these memories could eat me alive. A look, a touch, a kiss. They'll be burned into my brain forever.

Jarred pulls away first and laughs awkwardly. "Bye, Juniper."

My breath catches in my throat. "B-bye."

He grabs the last of their bags and goes out the front door without so much as looking back. I watch from the doorway as he settles into the car, wrapping my arms around me for warmth. The back window rolls down. Piper wears a smile on her tearstained face. "Don't take down the snowflakes!"

"I won't! I would never!" I call out.

Jarred waves at me from the driver's seat and they pull off down the driveway.

I stand there until the car is nothing but a speck, a memory.

I am alone again. And not just anyone can fill this void. I need Jarred. I *want* Jarred.

I walk back into the house. The huge empty house. It's just me now. I go into the living room and sit on the couch, looking up at the snowflakes hanging from the rafters. How did things happen so fast? How did they change in the blink of an eye?

What the hell have I done?

16

JARRED

From the moment we drove away from Hawthorn's Haven, I haven't been able to get June out of my head. She plagues my every waking moment. Hell, she plagues my every non-waking moment too.

It doesn't help that Piper is constantly talking about her. The whole ride home, she kept asking, "When will we see June again?"

"Soon, Pipes."

"Sunday dinner?"

I grimace at the thought. June isn't just a girl I can have a fling with and put squarely in the rearview mirror. She's a part of my family practically. *A sister*.

And yet, I keep having memories of kissing her. Her warm, cherry lips. Her hands working down my body. The way her mismatched eyes would flick into mine and cause a fire through my whole body. How will I be able to contain myself when I see her again? How will I be able to act as though nothing has happened between us?

When I walk into work on Monday morning, Dad

comes to find me almost immediately, eager to hear about the vacation.

"How was it?" he asks, plopping down in the chair across from my desk.

"Good." I open up my laptop and start going through emails.

A moment. "That's it? You've been gone for two weeks and all I get is a *good*?"

"Was part of the deal of my vacation that I had to write a report on it?" I ask drolly.

"No, but I thought—well, you must at least have some pictures of Piper, huh?"

I pause. I have a couple. But they're interspliced with pictures of Piper and June together, even before things escalated. I can't just hand over my phone and let him go through them. "Um. No. No pictures."

Dad frowns. "You didn't take *any* pictures? These are precious moments of your daughter's life and you're not recording them?!"

"I was just trying to be present and in the moment," I say. "Isn't that what you're always telling me to do? Be present or something."

He grunts. I know he can't resist that sort of self-improvement lingo. "I guess I'll just have to ask Piper about it."

Alarm bells go off in my head. I've done my best to cover my tracks with her, buying her loyalty with anything she wanted from the toy store yesterday. It wasn't as hard on my wallet as I thought it would be, mostly because she was enchanted by an old-fashioned, silver slinky more than anything else. She even named the thing Mr. Slinky and wanted to bring it to school this morning. "Don't!"

Dad's eyes widen. "Jeez, why not?"

I'm not being subtle, that's for damn sure. The whole situation, however, isn't subtle. June and I did something, lots of somethings that we shouldn't have. I'm going to try and cover it up like it's a crime scene. "It was just for me and her. It was supposed to be special. A memory just for us. You understand, don't you? Like when you used to take us camping and told us not to tell Mom."

Dad's face brightens at the mention of Mom. He nods, fondly remembering our times together. "The only reason I told you that is so you wouldn't tell her I let you all have candy for breakfast."

I laugh. "Is that why I've always had problems with cavities?"

"Listen, I can't be held responsible for cavities that may or may not have been caused by my indiscretion in the sugar department. Besides, they're good memories, aren't they?"

I nodded. I can always picture a memory clearly from one of those trips: Dad driving, me in the front seat, Oliver and Keifer crumpled over each other sleeping in the back. It's just a flicker of a memory, but it fills me with warmth. "I'm trying to create that for Piper. It's harder without any siblings for her. But I'm just trying to make it really special."

"I understand, bud."

I smile. Smoothed over, done and dusted. "How's Rye doing?"

Dad sighs, his eyes rolling to the side. "We're getting to that point that the beauty of pregnancy is about to turn into drudgery of pregnancy."

I nod as if I know, but I don't. The beauty of pregnancy was always lost on Meredith. She wanted it over before it began. I understand that now. "How much longer? A month?"

"Just about."

"You ready to have a baby again? Been a long time, hm?"

Dad shrugs. "I'm nervous, but I think it's a little like riding a bike. Plus, I had some practice with Piper. That helps."

We exchange a smile. "Let me know if I can do anything to help."

"Oh, no. No, no, no stay clear out of the way from my pregnant wife. She is a force to be reckoned with." Dad pushes himself out of his chair. "Okay, I'll check in later. Get settled in."

He gives me a smile over his shoulder and then leaves my office. I can finally breathe a sigh of relief. Then, I'm hit with the terrible thought: I'm going to have to do a lot of lying to make sure no one knows about me and June *ever*.

———

"Daddy?"

"Yes, Pipes."

Piper is sitting in front of the television watching a movie while I try and catch up on work. It's not the kind of quality time I prefer, but it's better than sticking her with a babysitter late into the night.

"Could we invite June to watch a movie with us?"

I stop typing abruptly and look up at her over my reading glasses. "You want her to watch a movie with us?"

Piper smiles: so innocent and uncomplicated. Little does she know how complicated the world really is.

"I don't know, honey... June's very busy."

She frowns. "But doesn't she have fun?"

"Sometimes."

"So, she can have fun with me!" she chirps excitedly.

I purse my lips. I can't be alone with June. It's proven too powerful. Even with Piper around, it's been proven we can't ignore the tension between us. But my daughter's hopeful little look is too powerful to bear. "Maybe. At the very least, we'll see her at Sunday dinner this week. You two can watch a movie after dinner if she's feeling up to it."

I can tell this answer doesn't really suit her, but something happens on the television that's too exciting to ignore. Her attention shifts completely. It's like our conversation never happened.

However, I can't just shift my attention as easily as that. Any time she mentions June, I'm stuck on the thought of her like a broken record that's repeating the same phrase over and over. *June... June... June...*

Would it be so bad if I reached out? Would it even be so bad if we tried to make something work in the real world, not in our winter hideaway? Maybe I could take her on one date and see how we feel. Maybe the chemistry isn't there beyond one date.

Who am I kidding, of course it is. June is like the sun thawing the earth as the season changes to spring. Like crocuses poking their heads through the soil. It's like her goal in life is to make everyone smile.

She's beautiful, inside and out.

Of course, there is the issue of my family. *Our* family in a sense. It would be a major betrayal. But... Clay got over Dad falling in love with his daughter. Any time I see them together, it's like nothing has changed. They've lived a lot more life than my brother has, though. Keifer can be so hotheaded, I think he might put me in traction if he found out I touched June.

Piper falls asleep in front of the television. I carry her up to her bed, relishing how her head fits into the crook of my neck, her soft, light brown hair tickling my cheek. I tuck her into bed, and she nestles in without much fuss. I kiss the top of her head, turn out the light, and leave her to her slumber.

I wish Piper had more than just me. That's a wish I've had since Meredith left. I wish she had a mother. Or a mother figure.

June could be that. I saw it with my own eyes. Her heart opened to my daughter without question. Am I taking away the opportunity for that kind of love from Piper? I'm older and wiser now. I can see better when people are genuine. Not like when I met Meredith. She was so enchanting I missed all the red flags. Now, looking at June, I'm pretty sure I am seeing her clearly.

But 'pretty sure' doesn't cut it. Not when Piper is involved. What if I'm missing something? Something that could break both our hearts all over again.

The thought of Piper losing someone else, especially now that she's older, is enough for me to close the book on June. We had our fun. I can hold onto the memories and look at them with fondness. That's all, though.

Juniper Reed is strictly off-limits. Permanently.

17

———

JUNE

Back at the homestead, my little house in Mayfair. The tenants left everything in surprisingly good shape. Thank God, because I can't afford to clean up after them. Especially now that I don't have a job.

My last few days at Hawthorn's Haven were nothing to write home about. It was sad to be there all on my own when the house had been filled with so much laughter and so much love.

Let me be clear. I know Jarred and I crossed a line we never should have crossed. But, fuck, I'm glad we did.

Not half an hour after I get home, I get a text from Keifer.

> Welcome home. I'll bring dinner. :)

Fuck, he must have checked my location on Find My Friends.

I'm not ready to face Keifer after everything that happened. He can always see right through me. The blessing and the curse of being best friends since childhood. We know each other too well.

However, this is self-preservation. There is no way in hell I'll let him know about me and Jarred. He didn't even know Jarred was there! I'll be in the clear if I can just act natural.

Keifer shows up around six with a bountiful bag of takeout from our favorite Thai restaurant. "Ahhh! I've missed you!" he yelps upon seeing me and wraps me up in a big hug.

"Keif, you're suffocating me," I manage to squeak out even though I can barely grab a breath in his embrace.

He releases me and holds up the bag. "Hungry?"

I smile. "Starving."

Keifer sets out all the takeout containers on the kitchen counter and retrieves two plates for us. He knows this house as well as I do, spent many hours playing in the basement and nights eating crappy food while my parents were working late. God, he really is like my brother. "So... how was it?"

"Great! It was really nice," I say with an irritated grin.

"Yeah?"

"Yeah. I owe you. Although I don't know if I have any favors as big as that."

Keifer laughs. "You don't owe me. Come on, let's eat."

We take our plates full of food and bring them into the living room. We always eat at the coffee table, just like when we were kids.

"Okay, so tell me more," Keifer says through a mouthful of chicken satay. "What'd you do with all your time?"

I poke my chopsticks around my pad see eiw, fishing out a piece of broccoli. "There's not really much to tell."

"Don't tell me you just watched TV the whole time."

I roll my eyes. "No, I didn't *just watch TV*. I was doing a lot of job searching. That's about it."

Keifer raises an eyebrow.

"What?"

"You're doing that thing."

"What thing?"

"When you're lying, your right cheek tremors."

I slap my hand to my right cheek. "No, it doesn't!"

"Yeah, it does!"

"Well, I'm not lying. There's no reason to. All I did was relax and take some time to myself. Too much time to myself. You know, I had so much alone time, you might as well call me a hermit. Or something like that." I'm rambling. Fuck, I always do that when I'm lying.

"Okay, okay! Nothing happened. Got it."

We eat in silence for a bit.

"You know, it was so weird, right when you left, Jarred disappeared too."

I resist every urge to drop my chopsticks in shock. "Oh?"

"Yeah! Turns out Dad gave him two weeks off without telling anyone. Apparently, Piper's going through something. Poor kid."

"Interesting... Do you know where he went?"

Keifer shakes his head. "Naw. I haven't talked to him about it yet."

My heart is pounding. Not only is he stressing me the fuck out with all his questions, but also the mention of Jarred has sent my body into heat. His face flashes in my mind. I can remember how he feels inside me. A panicked wave of arousal overcomes me for the briefest moment. I clutch the side of the table to steady myself. Keifer is *right fucking there*. If he could read my thoughts, I'd be so dead.

"You got that big storm, right?" Keifer asks.

"Yup."

"Did you get out okay? I was going to say you might need to call the plow company but kept forgetting."

Shit. When I'm lying, I try to leave out as many details as possible. Talking about the plow is *such* a detail. I hadn't accounted for this. Keifer isn't an idiot. It's his family's cabin for crying out loud. "I called them."

"Oh. Good."

I don't reply, instead stuffing my mouth with a potsticker so he can't get anything out of me even if he tried.

"Did you have enough food?"

I nod.

"Were you able to do laundry okay?"

I nod.

"You weren't too scared out there all on your own, were you?"

"Jesus, Keifer!" I shout. "Can you stop asking me questions for one fucking second?!"

Keifer blinks his light green eyes at me. They're different than Jarred's but the shape is like a photocopy. "What the hell, June? I'm just asking you about your life and you're being an asshole!"

"I'm not being an asshole! You're asking stupid questions!"

He gasps. "I'm asking stupid questions? I feel like I'm allowed a few, considering I let you stay at the cabin for two whole weeks."

I purse my lips together. I hate when he uses the money card. It just reminds me that no one thinks I can hack it on my own. Even me.

"I brought you dinner, I'm just trying to hang out with

you and talk and–" He stops and drops his chopsticks. "I'm not even hungry anymore."

"*Keifer...*"

He grabs his plate and goes into the kitchen. I stare at the space he left across the table. I didn't mean to make him mad. My guilt is getting in the way of just being normal. How the hell do I tame that? I get up and go to the doorway of the kitchen. He's washing his plate fiercely, scrubbing grime that is no longer there.

"I'm sorry."

Keifer doesn't respond. Great. The silent treatment.

"You know I'm so grateful that you gave me a place to stay," I go on, a knot in my throat. "I wish I could make it up to you, I don't mean to sound at all ungrateful."

He stops washing and puts the plate down in the sink, lowering his head. "I'm not trying to make you feel indebted, June." He raises his eyes to mine. His anger has dissipated. "I'm just really worried about you."

I straighten up. "You're worried about me?"

"Yeah. Of course, I am. Ever since you lost your job. And I barely heard from you the whole time you were gone... I've been worried."

I sigh. "I'm sorry. I didn't mean to make you worried. I'm stressed. I'm scared."

"I know you are." Keifer smiles sadly. "But you can't just bottle it all up."

Oh, I can, and I will. I'll bottle up everything that happened in Michigan until we've all forgotten about it. "You're right. I'm sorry."

"I just want to make sure you're okay."

My lip twitches. It starts as a grimace and turns into a smile. "I'm okay, Keif. Really." I glance at all the food still on the counter. "Now don't tell me you're actually full..."

"No," he grumbles. "I'm starving!"

I cackle. "Come on, let's finish dinner."

We can put it away tonight. But the truth is clear. I have to get a handle on this as soon as possible so that Keifer doesn't see through me ever again.

———

"Here, let me help you with that," I say to Rye, trying to cut her off from the oven.

"June, relax. You've helped with literally everything already. I can take something out of the oven," Rye replies, waving me off.

I step back and let her pull a casserole dish of asparagus out of the oven. It feels like she's gotten so big since the last time I saw her. It's only been a few weeks, but she looks like she could pop at any minute, even though she has a month left of her pregnancy.

"You know what you can do for me? You can grab a trivet and go put it on the dining room table."

"Got it. Which cabinet?"

Rye looks around the kitchen at all the cabinets. "God, I don't know. This place is still like a puzzle to me."

"I'll just open them all until I find them."

"But don't leave them open," Rye teases with a spoon. "Ash and the boys have this habit of leaving all the cabinets open. The last time they did that, I burst into tears."

"Rye..."

"Oh, don't pity me," she snorts. "I'm just..."

"Pregnant."

"Very," she replies, putting her hand on her belly. "And very nearly ready to not be."

I smile. "I'll find it, don't worry." I start to shuffle

through the cabinets looking for a trivet. Rye and I have become fast friends ever since she started coming to Sunday dinners last October. We bonded a lot, especially over Piper, who she was making a huge effort to get to know in preparation for impending motherhood.

Sometimes, though, I get a sinking feeling while looking at her. She's only a few years older than me, but she already seems to have her life sorted. Of course, I know it wasn't that simple. I only heard bits and pieces from Keifer about the drama that was Ash and Rye getting together. But she's stepped into her role as (the very young) matriarch of the Hawthorn family with ease and grace. She's married, having a baby, already planning out her flower business that's set to open in a year. Regardless of how it came to be, Rye has her shit together now.

I told her that once as I lamented being a directionless twenty-something and she just laughed. "You have no idea how fast things can change, June."

I try to remember that. But all that's changed so far is I lost my job and fucked my best friend's brother. Both are things that probably would have been better *not* happening.

"Dad sent me in to say 'hi'," Jarred's voice permeates the room.

The hair on the back of my neck stands up. I don't turn from the cabinet I'm searching.

"Would you not have said 'hi' if your dad hadn't told you to?" Rye asks teasingly.

"I didn't want to get in your way!"

"Is that a comment about me being pregnant? I resent that if it is."

I slowly turn around and watch Jarred and Rye hug lovingly. I wonder how Jarred feels that his dad's new wife is exactly his age. They seem to get on pretty well. When they part, Jarred's eyes jump to me. I try to smile but he looks away before I can. Ouch.

"Hey, June."

"Hi. How's it go—*oof!*" The wind is knocked out of me as Piper rams into me, giving me a great big hug.

"June! I've missed you!"

I cautiously wrap my arms around her. "Hi, Piper."

"That's so sweet," Rye says. "I didn't know Piper liked June so much."

"I *love* June, Gramma!" Piper announces with a grin, tucking her chin against my belly and looking up at me.

"Jarred, could you get everyone in the dining room? And send your father in to help me. Dinner's going to be ready in just a minute."

I don't even get a chance to talk with her before Jarred yanks her away from me. "Okay, honey, let's go sit and get ready for dinner."

I feel the absence of her presence through my whole body, an ache I didn't know was there. Jarred has this disentanglement easy compared to me. I have to forget about both him and Piper. How is that fair?

I quickly find the trivet and head off into the dining room where Jarred has managed to shepherd everyone. I plop the trivet down on the table and go directly to my spot next to Keifer. This is going way worse than I imagined it. I thought Jarred would be able to at least be pleasant with me, the way he always used to be. Now, it feels like he's punishing me for a secret that *he's* also a part of.

"You okay?"

I glare at Keifer. "Fine. Why?"

"You're completely flushed."

I touch my cheek. Warm. Fuck. That's embarrassing.

"Hot in the kitchen." I grab the glass of water at my spot and chug it.

The table is way quieter than it usually is as we wait for Ash and Rye to come out with the food. Trevor, Oliver's best friend, and his girlfriend, Rowan, have no expression on their faces. There's a chill in the air emanating from them. Usually, they're goofing off together. Something's off between them.

Oliver, consequently, is also keeping to himself, flipping his fork over and over.

And then there's Jarred, who has a steely look on his face, like he's a rock that needs to be chiseled. Piper's the only one with any sort of spirit and even she notices that the tone is completely different than usual. "It's so quiet..." she giggles.

"Just a quiet sort of night, I guess." Jarred crosses his arms over his chest. He's intent on keeping it that way.

I purse my lips and then lean in Piper's direction. "You want to play a game, Piper?"

Her eyes brighten. "What kind of game?"

"It's called 'I'm going on a picnic.'"

Rowan awakens at this moment. "Oh, *loved* this game."

"So, Piper, you'll start. You'll say, 'I'm going on a picnic and I'm bringing *blank*'. But the blank has to be something that starts with the letter 'a'."

Piper looks around the table, taking in her surroundings as she thinks. "I'm going on a picnic, I'm going to bring an... anteater!"

Everyone laughs. Except Jarred. He doesn't even crack a smile.

"Interesting picnic! Okay, now, Keifer, you repeat what Piper's said and add another item. *Except* it has to start with 'b'."

Keifer smiles and nods. "Okay, okay got it. I'm going on a picnic and I'm bringing an anteater and a... um..."

"Box," Oliver interrupts.

"Shut up, man! I'm thinking! Um..."

"Berry bush," Oliver interrupts again.

Keifer balls up his napkin and throws it at him. Piper laughs wildly. "Let me think! Um... I'm bringing a brick."

"Then me! I'm going on a picnic and I'm bringing an anteater, a brick, and a clown!"

Piper is in hysterics. We keep going around the table, Trevor, Rowan, and Oliver adding their words respectively.

"Dagger."

"Elephant."

"Floss."

Once it gets to Jarred, he glances around the table, completely unamused. "Pass."

Before anyone can question him, Piper's standing on her chair, enthusiastically crying out, "I'm going on a picnic and I'm bringing an anteater, a brick, a clown, a dagger, an elephant, floss, and a golden pony!"

"Piper, sit down." Jarred tries to pull her down, but she resists.

"Why do you have such a stick up your you-know-what, Jarred?" Keifer asks.

"I don't have a stick up my–"

"Then why aren't you playing along? It's rude to–" Oliver tries to cut in.

"Oh, please, I'm a grown man, I don't want to participate in some stupid game."

Piper gasps in alarm. "That's a bad word, Daddy!"

"Yeah. And it's rude to June. She was just trying to pass the time and keep *your* kid occupied."

"Keifer, it's fine," I try to intercede, but I know where

this is going. When the Hawthorns start to squabble, we're in for a war.

"Well, who *said* June needed to keep Piper occupied? I didn't ask. Maybe she shouldn't stick her nose where it doesn't belong. My daughter was just fine before June had to take it upon herself to involve everyone at this table without caring about what other people wanted. Who does she think she is? Just because she thinks she's some sort of child whisperer? Well, I'm not a child, so I don't have to abide by Ms. Reed's moods."

Where did *that* come from? I'm too stunned to defend myself. Thankfully, Oliver and Keifer are more than willing to fight on my behalf.

"What the he... heck, man?" Oliver says.

"Completely uncalled for. Apologize."

Jarred looks away, his lips sewn together.

"Wow, really mature. The silent treatment. Your daughter is sitting right there, you need to set an example for her. Apologize to June."

"I just said it was a dumb game!"

"No, you used the s-word, Daddy," Piper corrects. Gotta hand it to her, she really knows how to hold her own in situations like this.

"Exactly!" Keifer shouts. "You were really rude. Apologize *now*."

I shake my head. This couldn't have gone worse. I shouldn't be here. I look across the table at Jarred. His blue-green eyes meet mine for a brief moment. There's no kindness in them. Just... frustration. Anger? "This is bullshit," Jarred mutters, then slams his hands on the table to push himself to standing. He tears out of the room without another word.

Everyone is silent, in disbelief. Jarred rarely loses his

temper. It's a scary thing to see. Fortunately, Piper doesn't seem phased. "Yeesh. What's eating him?"

I try to laugh. She must have heard that on some television show or something. It's too out of the ordinary. But I can't. If I laugh too hard, I think I might cry. What have I done?

"What the hell is wrong with him?" Keifer growls.

"Keif, please– "

Oliver pushes his chair out from the table. "I'll go talk to him." He comes over to me and touches my arm, a sympathetic look in his eye. An apology. I appreciate it more than I can say, but inside, if I'm honest, it doesn't count for much unless it's coming from Jarred himself.

As soon as Oliver walks out of the room, Ash and Rye enter carrying dishes of food, both of them glowing with laughter. "Dinner!" Rye announces, but when she takes in the mood of the room, her smile fades. "Is everything alright?"

No one is willing to respond.

"Where's Jarred? And Oliver?" Ash asks. For some reason, he's looking at me. As if I have an answer for this.

I don't want to be here. I have to get out. Or else, I'll explode.

18

JARRED

I prepared all day for the moment I'd see June. I told myself over and over that it would be fine. I'd be able to ignore our dirty little secret and put our attraction behind us. But from the moment I saw her in the kitchen, my heart has been racing. Something short-circuited in my brain. I could picture her naked, her beautiful body wanting for my touch.

I can't seem to catch my breath.

I go right from the dining room to the office. I'll get some peace and quiet there. I pace the floor, hand to my chest, hoping this will stop the pounding.

Fuck, what have I done?

I felt like a cornered wolf at the dinner table. I was just trying to keep things ordinary. I thought I'd be able to slip into the background, but no one was talking and then, June being June, she comes up with this game to keep Piper happy.

I was a complete dick. But I couldn't help it. I needed to protect myself. I think I may have over-corrected, pushed her away forcefully. Now, I ended up making myself the center of attention.

"You're such an idiot, Jare," I say to myself. I slap my hand to my forehead. On top of all of this, Piper was sitting right there, watching me be utterly abhorrent to a person she loves.

Loves. She had said it at the cabin, and she just said it right there in the kitchen. She loves June.

How could I be so fucking naïve? Putting this affair behind us is going to be near impossible when Piper has all these memories of June caring for her.

"Hey, what the fuck?"

I turn around to find Oliver in the doorway of the office. "Leave me alone, man."

"No, what the hell was that? You don't talk to June like that. *No one* talks to June like that."

I shake my head. "I didn't say anything *to* June."

"Oh, right, sorry. You talked shit about her right in front of her face. There's a difference." Oliver rolls his eyes. "What's gotten into you?"

What the fuck do I say to him? How do I answer his question? There's no logical reason I can use as an explanation. Not really. "I'm stressed. Catching up with all the work this week—"

"Bullshit. That's a lame excuse."

I grit my teeth. *Don't snap, Jarred. Do not snap.* "What do you want me to say?"

"I just want to understand what you think gave you the right to do that?"

I don't respond. I lean against the big hardwood desk and screw my forehead together to think harder. At least to pretend to think harder for Oliver's benefit.

"June's like our sister, Jare," Oliver says in a soft and gentle voice.

She's not like our sister. Not to me. Not at all. People

don't *fuck* their sisters. People don't picture their sisters naked. People don't want their sisters.

That's what it boils down to.

I still want June. With every fiber of my being.

"And for you to not even apologize –"

"I'm sorry. I don't know what got into me."

"Don't apologize to me! Go out there and apologize to her."

I glance at the door of the office and then at the tips of my shoes. I can't move a muscle. I can picture the apology going down. I'd approach her, look down into her eyes and immediately lose myself in them. I'd want to kiss her and that feeling would be too painful to survive.

Jesus, how old am I? Nearly thirty but acting like a fucking teenager who's touched a boob for the first time. This is pathetic.

"What's going on, Jarred? Seriously."

I swallow. "It's hard to watch someone be so good with Piper when I'm..." I feel tears creep into my eyes. This isn't a lie. It's the cold hard truth. Just a few facts omitted. "...when I'm all she's got. You know?"

Oliver sighs and nods. "I thought that was it."

Thank God.

Oliver sits on the desk beside me. Nearly a head taller than me, people always assume he's the older one. And since we're only a year apart, sometimes he acts like it. "You are an amazing dad, Jarred."

"Most of the time," I say with a sad chuckle.

"Well, no one's an amazing anything a hundred percent of the time." Oliver wraps his arm around my shoulder. "I get it. Piper deserves a mom. Of course, she does. But the way things shook out with Meredith, that wasn't in your control."

I shut my eyes, a tear rolling down my cheek.

"You have to let people help when they can."

I've gotten better at accepting help over the years. But it's not about help. It's that when I see how Piper and June interact, I can see the next twenty years playing out, the two of them together. June's been more of a mother to Piper than Meredith ever was, ever *could* be.

And I have to sit there at the dinner table and watch something so amazing slip right out of my grasp. It hurts too much to bear.

"Don't let Piper watch you push help away. That can't be good for her."

"I know. I know, it was—it was wrong, I get it. I'll apologize. I just hope I haven't hurt June's feelings too much."

Oliver smiles. "June's family, Jarred."

Knife to the heart.

"She'll forgive you. No problem."

The door to the office flies open, revealing a red-faced Keifer. "I hope you're happy, jackass."

"Keifer, it's all settled. Jarred is going to apologize."

Keifer laughs bitterly. "June left."

I get to my feet. "What?!"

"I begged her not to and said you just needed a minute, but she thought she was getting in the way and just walked out."

I push past Keifer and go to the front door. "No. I need to apologize."

"Too little, too late."

I open the front door, mid-February chill scraping against my face. I count the cars in the driveway: one, two, three, four...

There should be five.

She left. She really left.

And it's all my fault.

"She doesn't want to talk to you."

I turn around to face Keifer. His face is rigid with fury.

"So stay the fuck away from her. Got it?"

Keifer has a temper, that's always been obvious. But he's never managed to intimidate me. Not until now. "Got it."

If Keifer is this mad at me for driving June away from dinner, then one thing is abundantly clear: he can *never* find out what happened between us.

19

———

JUNE

"Come on, June. This is the third time you've said no." Keifer sounds so sad I almost change my mind.

"I'm sorry, Keif. I have plans." It's not a total lie. I have a date with the television tonight. In front of me, an episode of some Real Housewives show is paused while Keifer begs me to come to Sunday dinner over the phone.

"You're never this busy," he grumbles.

I laugh. "Hey! You should be happy I have plans. You're always telling me I'm a hermit."

"Well, you are. You work too hard."

I grimace. Haven't been working too hard lately. I've gone on several interviews with families who need new nannies. Two didn't give me a call back, one I didn't call back. I tried to get back in touch with the agency I was a part of, but my old family gave me such a terrible review that they have banned me from the agency for a whole year.

I should have given the *family* a scathing review. But I didn't have the gumption to. I was too heartbroken.

"Please, June. Just an hour."

"Keifer, I can't."

He's silent for a moment. I can almost hear his cogs shifting as he tries to decide what to say. "If this is because of Jarred, then –"

"It's not because of Jarred, Keifer." It is *completely* because of Jarred.

"He'll leave you alone, I promise."

That's not exactly what I want. It's the opposite. I want things to be good between us. At the deepest part of me, I want things to go back to the way they were at the cabin. Not the sex, although I'd love that. I want the intimacy. The familiarity. The moments between the kisses where we looked into each other's eyes and saw...

I saw a future. I don't know if he saw the same thing.

"Piper misses you. She's always asking for you."

I shut my eyes tight. Keifer thinks that's helping. He has no idea that just makes it worse. "Tell her I miss her."

"I will."

"And give everyone my love. Especially Rye. I know she needs it." Rye and I text often. Now that her baby is due in just a week, her texts have become less frequent. I miss her.

God, I'm lonely.

"I will, June." Keifer pauses. "Movie sometime this week?"

I smile. "Sure."

"Cool. Have fun with your *plans*."

"Don't say that like they're not real!"

"Whatever!"

Keifer hangs up. I can't help but laugh. He knows me too well. At least he can respect I don't want to go.

To be honest, though, I don't know if I'll ever be ready to go back. The more time I've spent away from them, the more I feel like I've betrayed the Hawthorns, at least the ones I haven't screwed. Why would they welcome me back into their life when I've abandoned them?

This might be a good thing. A clean break. Truth is, though I love them, I don't *need* them. I need myself. I need to work on getting a job and making a life and cleaning the house, and you know what? It might be a perfect time for a dog.

Goddamn, I'm lonely.

I lie there in front of the TV for a while until my head starts to hurt. I've been feeling so sluggish lately. Like crap. I'm not eating very well, and I've been drinking more often since I don't have anywhere to be in the mornings. Might be time to pay closer attention to that.

I know what will help. A shower.

I march myself up the stairs, strip, and get into the shower. The water feels wondrous over my body, caressing all the parts of me that have felt stale after spending a day in musty sweatpants. My eyes flutter shut as the warmth overcomes me.

I've never been touch-starved in my life, but ever since sleeping with Jarred, I miss being close to him. To feel his heat, his breath in my ear, his body curled around mine. I'd never felt so safe and protected in my life and that includes when I was a kid. I've always felt like everyone's got one foot out the door.

His face flashes in my mind, the face he makes when he's about to tumble over the edge. His pretty lips parted, releasing a gasp, his eyelids drooping down so the blue green of his irises are mere slivers, his hair piecey with sweat.

Arousal cartwheels up my body. My eyes shoot open. I have to brace myself on the shower wall.

I need him *out* of my mind. Not in it.

I move the faucet handle all the way to cold and let out a screech.

———

"Juniper..."

My body is rocking back and forth.

"Juniper..."

Hands traveling down from my waist to my thighs.

"Beautiful, Juniper."

Lips on my collarbone. On my neck.

Him.

I wrap my arms around Jarred. The expanse of his back is just like I remember: sturdy and wide. I rock with him, but I can't feel him inside. Not yet. He's preparing me, teasing me, taunting me.

I love it.

Jarred moves his lips to meet mine. Tastes the same.

"What are we doing?" My voice is hoarse, almost as if I'm not speaking.

"What we're meant to do, Juniper."

I push my body up to meet his. I've missed him. This month since we've been together has been hell. I want him. I need him. I slide my hands down his back to his waist and try to map out every square inch of his topography. I don't want to forget this time. I want my nerve endings to be able to replay this moment forever.

"I should've stayed."

I whimper.

"I shouldn't have left you there."

I wrap my hands around his head and play with the long locks of his hair, just as soft as I remember. Jarred is nearly an extension of my body. How could we have abandoned each other? How could we have sacrificed our happiness for everyone else's comfort.

Then we're interrupted by the sound of Keifer's voice. "Hey!"

Jarred's lips part from mine.

I look in the direction of the voice. But Keifer isn't there.

"What the hell, June."

In horror, I turn back to Jarred and find myself face to face with Keifer. His anger is palpable, so hot I can feel it on my face. He pushes his face closer and closer to mine, teeth bared like he might eat me. *What the hell have you done?*

———

I wake up with a gasp like I'm coming up from water. My bedroom is still dark. It must be the middle of the night. I'm covered in sweat and my head is pounding.

Thank God it was just a dream.

I put my hands over my eyes. Fuck, I've really got to stop eating fried food. I flop a hand over onto my bedside table, grab a bottle of Advil and pop two in my mouth before collapsing back into my pillow.

Goddammit. Jarred Hawthorn is going to haunt me forever, isn't he?

JARRED

The office has been... tense. To put it delicately. Usually, my brothers and I have conflict at work and are all good at home. Not the other way around.

We work really hard not to bring work home with us. But personal life isn't the same. I've never found a good way of checking that at the door.

Even though it's been over a month since that fateful family dinner, Keifer is still holding a grudge against me. I can't help it that June doesn't want to come to family dinners anymore. And I'd be going against Keifer's explicit wish that I don't speak to her if I reached out and tried to encourage her to come.

At first, I thought it was good she wasn't there. Then I wouldn't have reason to think about her. But I was kidding myself. I always have reason to think about June. Even when I'm trying to focus on other things, she's only a thought away. Sometimes, I conjure a memory, other times it's just the thought of her beautiful smile. I can't get her out of my head. Missing her is slowly killing me.

It mostly happens around Piper. She asks about her

from time to time and has been less than lively at our family dinners when she realizes June won't be there. Everyone does their best to keep her entertained, but Dad and Rye are distracted by the impending arrival of their baby and Rowan and Trevor are distracted by the impending demise of their relationship (don't tell Oliver I said that, but it seems more than obvious from their near inability to have a civil conversation that doesn't involve another person).

I'm doing my best for her. But again, I always feel like I'm coming up short.

I get an email notification while dissociating at my desk. From Keifer. I sigh. The guy has an office right across from mine and he won't just come over and talk to me.

I open the email.

Subject Line: You type too loud.

And the body of the email is empty.

This is getting ridiculous. Not only are we constantly at odds with each other these days, but he's also being a jerk about everything. I'm not going to stand for this any longer. There's no reason that we should be at odds. The June thing is behind us. Why can't he just grow a pair and move on?

It doesn't help on top of everything that Dad has been at the hospital since the night before, waiting for his new baby to be born. We're all on pins and needles, waiting for the call that everything's gone fine and we need to rush over and meet her. Until then, though, we worry.

I get up from my desk and walk directly into his office without knocking. He looks up from his computer with an annoyed look. "Do you mind?"

"Do *you* mind?"

We stare at each other. Ah, the pains of working with family. The arguments can be so juvenile.

"I'm a busy man, Jarred. You could have walked in on an important, private meeting."

"Is that what you call drafting a fantasy basketball team?"

Keifer rolls his eyes and leans back in his chair. "You're so childish, Jarred."

"Me?! You're the one sending emails when I'm literally across the hall. Not to mention the subject matter is what I would call rather childish. My *typing* is too loud for you? What kind of bullshit is that?"

Keifer shrugs. His expression is so nonplussed it makes me want to punch him in the jaw. "It's too loud. What else do you want from me?"

"Look, if this is all about June –"

"*This isn't about June,*" he spits at me. "It's about how loud you type. It's obnoxious."

I stare at him. "You're obnoxious."

"*You're* obnoxious. I can hear you press the enter key like it's a fucking bomb detonating. Click, click, click! It's annoying."

"Our doors are closed! How can you – "

"I have misophonia. It's a sensitivity to sound."

"Oh my gooooooood. That's not even a thing! That's just a way for you to blame every time you're annoyed on someone or something else rather than focusing on the fact that you're being a little bitch!"

Keifer stands up and approaches me. My little brother has a couple inches on me, but it doesn't intimidate me in the least. "You want to take this outside?"

"You too afraid to fight me here?"

"No, I just don't want you to be embarrassed when you give up."

Suddenly, Oliver bursts through the door. "Guys! We have to get to the hospital!"

The tension dissipates like air out of a balloon. Keifer and I split apart.

"Did it happen? Is she here?" Keifer asks anxiously.

"Get your coats. We've got a baby to meet."

———

The guys and I pile into the car and first go pick Piper up from school. When I tell her that we're going to meet Grampa's new baby, she is over the moon, bouncing wildly in her car seat the whole way to the hospital.

"I can't wait to meet her!"

Neither can I.

On the ride from the school to the hospital, Keifer makes a phone call. "Hey. If you're free, you should meet us at the hospital... yeah, just a bit ago, apparently."

I can hear a voice talking excitedly on the other end of the phone.

"Yeah, of course, I'm sure! Rye will want to see you... Okay, okay, okay," Keifer chuckles. "We'll see you there." He hangs up. "Well, June's excited."

I feel a lump in my throat.

"June's coming?" Piper asks excitedly.

"Yeah! Isn't that exciting?" Keifer glares back at me from the front seat. "Unless *you* have a problem with that?"

My heart starts galloping in my chest. "N-no problem. Just thought this was a family only sort of thing."

His eyes harden in mine. Green, a spitting image of Dad's. He can strike fear in me with the echo of our father. "June *is* family. Besides. She wouldn't let me live it down if I didn't at least invite her."

"Hey, Piper, don't you love this song?!" Oliver turns up the radio. Something by Olivia Rodrigo (or at least I think that's her name). Only a second later, the car is filled with the sound of Piper attempting to sing along very, very loudly.

It isn't until we get to hospital and get out of the car that Keifer and I speak again. "Don't talk to her unless you're going to apologize," he says in a low, threatening voice.

"Got it."

Clay and Giselle, Rye's father and stepmother, are already waiting in the lobby holding a ginormous bouquet. Giselle is also expecting, sporting a burgeoning bump. Must be something in the air these days.

We greet each other, but my mind is a million miles away, anticipating June's arrival. *Don't talk to her unless you're going to apologize.* Can I say "hello" or will that upset Keifer too? Last thing I need is the two of us getting into a scrap outside Rye's hospital room.

Luckily, when June arrives, everyone else makes up for my silence. Piper rushes over to her and embraces her and Keifer is immediately at her arm. I'm assuming he's trying to protect her from me.

If only he knew the truth.

Even if I had to speak to June, I don't know if I could. Her beauty takes the words right out of my mouth. Her face is bare of makeup and her auburn hair falls in soft waves over her shoulders. More than any woman I've ever seen, June encapsulates what it means to be a natural beauty. She lights up the room with her smile, still so easy even though things are so complicated.

Piper doesn't want to leave her side, asking for June to pick her up. I want to refuse in a genteel way, but Keifer gives me a look that shakes me to my core. *Fine.*

Everything dissipates once Dad comes down and tells us that Rye and the new baby, Ivy, are happy and healthy. I'm over the moon. Clay and Giselle go up ahead of us.

I can't help glancing at June from time to time. With Piper on her hip, she looks exactly like a mother, and it stirs something in me. That primal desire to claim her the way she's let me before. It's so wrong that these are my primary feelings while meeting my baby sister, but I can't help it. When June is around, I can't think straight.

We go up a bit later and meet little Ivy. Rye is glowing, happy to see us all and well-recovered from her labor. Each of us meet baby Ivy, but it's Piper's meeting that captures all of our attention. She climbs up on the bed and stares down at the baby with complete awe.

I wish I could give her a little brother or sister. She'd be so good at it. So utterly thrilled to be the responsible, older child.

I find my eyes traveling to June. She's teary-eyed, her hands folded nervously in front of her. I wait for her to notice me looking. To let me know things might be okay between us. That we can get through this.

Her mismatched eyes find mine. The joy in her face dissipates and her nostrils flair.

I look away. That's as clear a message as any.

June wants nothing to do with me. And as much as I don't want to admit it, it breaks my heart in two.

21

———

JUNE

"What about this? Family of four seeking spirited, excited nanny who can plan activities and help kids with learning," Keifer reads off his computer. "Must be able to drive, have CPR certification, and a good attitude."

The two of us have been prowling postings all morning. It's not going well.

I raise my eyebrow. "What's the compensation?"

Keifer scans the page. Then, his jaw drops. "Twelve dollars an hour?! That's –"

"That's how they always get you. It's the bit about having a good attitude. You always know they're going to be cheapskates."

"That's not even minimum wage! How is that even legal!"

I shrug. "A lot of people work off the books. Everyone wants someone amazing to work with their children but some aren't willing to pay for it. It's the whole racket."

"Racket is right. Jesus..."

My eyes are starting to hurt from staring at a computer screen. "Look, nothing good is really going to become available until the end of the school year. I might just have to bide my time."

Keifer sighs. "Could you... maybe..."

"What?"

"What if you went back to your old family? Asked for your job back."

I purse my lips together.

"I can't imagine you could have done anything so bad as to merit firing."

My eyes meet Keifer's briefly and then skitter away. I haven't told him how it all shook out with the old family. In fact, I haven't told anyone. There's no reason to. It's in the past. And I don't want to dredge it up. "I can't do that."

"But–"

"Keifer, I can't, alright?" I reply firmly. "It's done. We're done with them."

He shuts up at that. I'm not usually forceful, but I can't continue that conversation. Too much pain on top of all the rest of the pain I've experienced over the past month and a half.

"What are you going to do for money until then?" he asks from the silence.

I eye him. I know what he's about to say, so I head him off at the pass. "I'll manage."

"Because I can help if you–"

"I don't want your money, Keifer."

"I know you don't. That's not what this is about." Keifer closes his computer and leans forward. "I know you can't afford the upkeep of the house without steady work."

I swallow. God, I've been hiding so much from him since the beginning of this year. The reason my job ended, my affair with Jarred, now *this*. I need to take one thing off my plate, so I don't feel like such a terrible friend. "I can use my savings until I get back on my feet."

"June... no, I can't let you do that."

"Yes. You can. You're going to have to. Because I'm not accepting a cent from you." Maybe a year ago I would have. But now that I've betrayed Keifer over and over again, I can't even begin to imagine taking his help in that way. It would feel like taking advantage. I fuck his brother and then he gives me a loan? Yeah, right.

"June, you're my best friend. You can have a loan and then some. You know it's no skin off my back. Really."

I close my eyes and shake my head. "Keifer, can we drop this for now?"

He starts to say something but thinks better of it. "Yeah. Yeah. We can drop it."

I rub my temples, trying to make the pressure dissipate. "You okay?"

"Just a headache. I've been getting them a lot lately."

Keifer sighs. "Too much stress, probably."

He comes over to where I'm sitting and holds out his hand. "What's that for?"

"Take it. We're gonna go for a walk."

Mayfair has always been a good walking neighborhood. Lots of families and schools, parks to mill around in, lots of friendly dogs. I have so many memories of pounding the pavement with Keifer when we were just kids. Now, we're adults. And life...

Life sucks. It's too hard. Everything you read, every movie you see makes it seem like life has a way of working itself out. It doesn't. You fuck your best friend's brother, and you suffer because on one hand, you betrayed your friend, and on the other, you can't stop thinking about his brother.

It's a bitterly cold late-March day. March in Chicago is worse than the depths of January because we all become desperate for spring and every cold day feels like Mother Nature giving us a big "fuck you."

I have my arm linked in Keifer's. We've been mistaken for a couple on a few occasions. But it's just a friendly closeness we've always had. I know I'm not Keifer's type. And he thinks he's not mine, although how can I really say that when I pine after Jarred nonstop?

"Have you talked to Rye recently?"

"Oh, yeah! I meant to show you." Keifer whips his phone out and pulls up a picture of Ivy. "Almost two weeks old."

The newborn baby girl is scrunched up amidst plush looking blankets, peacefully asleep. "Look at that angel..."

"That's not what Dad would tell you," Keifer laughs. "He hasn't gotten a wink of sleep since she's been born. I think he's being dramatic." He puts his phone away, but I'm still left with the image of that dear little baby.

When I saw her in the hospital, Rye holding her and Ash looking on with pride and adoration, I felt a pull in the pit of my stomach. A reminder that something in my life is missing. Whether or not that's a baby, I don't know. But, damn, it looked nice. And Jarred being there too with Piper filled me with a rush of feeling.

Could we have that? I've wondered every day since.

"I've been meaning to reach out to Rye, but I don't want to overwhelm her."

Keifer pats my arm. "Just let her know you're thinking of her. I know she'll appreciate that."

I didn't see Rye at all before Ivy was born, having

ditched every family dinner I could. I feel guilty for not being there. My own cowardice got in the way of supporting my friend at the most tender moment of her life.

"I'd send flowers, but she's the flower queen, so..."

"Honestly, I think you could send a pack of diapers and she'd be over the moon."

I laugh and squeeze Keifer tighter. I'm so lucky to have him. I don't know what I'd do if I...

The tension in my head starts to morph. It's not pain anymore. But dizziness.

"June? You okay?"

"Yeah... yeah, I'm just a little dizzy."

We take a few more steps. I feel my knees buckle. The world starts spinning in front of my eyes until all the colors mush together into black. The last thing I hear is Keifer crying out my name.

———

My mouth feels dry. I'm laid on my back, being moved somewhere. I blink my eyes open and see a low ceiling. I'm in a car. An ambulance. Holy shit.

"There she is."

"Where... what's going on?" I croak out.

"June! June, it's me. It's Keifer." I feel his hand interlace in mine and turn my head toward him. He looks like a fucking wreck with tears in his eyes. He's shaking. "Oh god, I was so worried."

"What happened?"

"You passed out. I had to call an ambulance."

I look down my arm. There's an IV sticking out of the back of my hand. "What? I... I fainted?"

"Yeah, while we were walking." He pats my hand.

"Don't worry about a thing. We're headed to the hospital now."

I can't believe my ears. How did this happen? "It's okay. I don't need to go to the hospital."

Keifer tries to laugh. "Too late. We're headed there now." He squeezes my hand. "I've got you covered. You know, all the payments. It's okay."

"No, no. I'm just stressed. There's nothing wrong with me." I can't afford for anything to be wrong with me. Literally and figuratively. "I promise, this is all just a–"

I feel a hand on my shoulder as I try to sit up. One of the EMTs, a woman with a clicked back brown bun. "Relax, ma'am. Just lay back. There's no reason to get too excited."

I look to Keifer in alarm. For help. Something.

"If nothing's wrong, then nothing's wrong. But it's better to be safe than sorry," he says. I can tell by his voice that there's no room for argument.

I don't respond. I just lay back and let the people around me take control. For once, I'll let them take control.

———

"Please stop pacing."

"I'm nervous."

"It's my body. I'm the one who should be nervous."

We're in a room at the hospital. Keifer is pacing back and forth while I sit in a hospital bed. We're waiting for blood work to come back and a urine sample and any other number of tests. I've been asked so many questions I don't even know which way is up.

I feel fine now. Completely normal. But Keifer is too nervous. It's like he's my dad, or something. He wants to make sure nothing is wrong and insisted on almost every possible test that wouldn't require some outrageous machine.

There's a knock on the door. Keifer hops to attention and opens it before the doctor can announce his presence. "Hi, doctor."

The doctor, an older, balding gentleman, smiles. "Well, hello. I'm Dr. Oppenheim. You're not Ms. Reed, are you?" he asks wryly.

Keifer blushes and steps aside. "No, no. Sorry."

"I am."

Dr. Oppenheim looks to me. By the warmth he's exuding, he either has great news or really horrible, life altering news. "I have some good news, Ms. Reed. Your blood work came back fine. All the tests we did show that you're perfectly healthy."

I sigh in relief. "Thank god."

"You did have one abnormality in your samples, though."

My gut twists. Dr. Oppenheim is still smiling. He looks *jolly* even. How can he be jolly about an abnormality?

"Although in my opinion, it's one of the most normal abnormalities a woman could have." He looks to Keifer and then back to me. "Congratulations. You're expecting."

What?

"Expecting? Like a... like a baby?" Keifer asks.

Dr. Oppenheim chuckles. "Yes. Exactly like a baby."

Keifer backs up into a chair along the wall and collapses into it.

"You're handling it really well for a dad-to-be, I promise."

There is no way that I'm pregnant. No fucking way. I'm on birth control. And sure, it malfunctions sometimes, but I can't be pregnant. Because the only guy I've had sex with in the past six months is Jarred Hawthorn and if I'm pregnant and I only slept with Jarred Hawthorn, then that means–

"From the quantitative blood test we did, I think you're about a month and a half to two months along. Everything's looking okay. We can do an ultrasound if you like to have a clearer picture..." Dr. Oppenheim glances between Keifer and me. "But I can tell this might be surprising to hear so maybe I'll come back and let you guys digest the news together and we can talk about how to proceed. Alright?"

I nod. "Thank you, doctor."

He gives me one last smile and leaves.

The room is deathly silent. Keifer sits and stares at his hands. It's not even his baby, but he's certainly acting like it is from how terror has stricken his body.

The news is starting to settle. I'm pregnant. Well, looks like what happens in the cabin doesn't always stay in the cabin. And if I don't handle this soon, it's going to be impossible to cover up. Emotions flood through me. I want to cry in both sadness and happiness at once.

"A month and a half to two months. That's exactly when you were at the cabin."

My reverie breaks. I look over at Keifer. His stare is so intense I feel like a bug that's been pinned down by a scientist.

"Did you have some sort of... one-night stand or meet someone out there?"

I can't do this. I can already hear the betrayal in his voice. He's already hurt that I didn't tell him something happened out there. It's only going to get worse when I tell him the truth.

But I have to. I have to tell him.

Before I can speak, I burst into tears. He starts to come

toward me to comfort me. "June, it's going to be okay. I promise it will be."

I hold up my hands. "Wait. I need to tell you something. And it's going to be hard to hear."

Keifer frowns. "Okay."

Breathe in. Breathe out. Spill.

"Jarred was at the cabin."

Keifer's expression doesn't change. "What?"

"He arrived after I got there. With Piper. And we decided we would both stay and it wouldn't be a big deal. But the longer we were there..."

Recognition passes over him.

"It just happened," I say in a tear-clogged whisper.

Keifer takes a step back from me. I can feel his hurt just as viscerally as he does. "Once?"

I could lie again, but I've already gotten this far.

"It just happened once, *right?*"

I shake my head.

"Oh my god."

"Only at the cabin! I promise. Not since then."

Keifer turns away and starts to pace again. "Oh my fucking god, this explains so much."

"Please don't be mad..."

"Are you kidding? I'm fucking furious!"

I purse my lips. More tears stream down my face.

"You two have just been hiding this dirty little secret, pretending like everything is normal when... everything has changed."

"Nothing's changed, Keifer. I promise, nothing."

"You're *pregnant,* June! How can you say nothing's changed when there's evidence of everything right in this fucking room?"

I descend into hysterics. I knew he'd be mad, but right

now, when I'm such a mess, I can't handle it. "Please don't yell at me, please don't be mad…" I repeat over and over.

Keifer doesn't say another word. He comes over to me and wraps his arms around me. Even though he's upset, he's still my best friend. He holds me for a while. "What do you want to do, June?"

"I don't know. I can't tell Jarred. He can't know. Please don't say anything."

"Of course, I won't."

Our eyes meet. His green eyes are swimming with tears I know he won't let fall. How could I do this to him? And how is he still so brave to sit here with me and put his feelings aside to support me?

"I don't even know if I want to keep it or not."

"That's okay. You have time to think about it."

I chew on the inside of my cheek. "If I keep it, though, Jarred won't be a part of it."

Keifer's brow furrows. "Are you sure?"

"He's made it clear he wants nothing to do with me. We all know that. This would just make everything worse."

He nods and wraps his hand around the back of my neck. "Hey. I got you. You're not going to do this alone. I promise."

I don't know what I did to deserve a friend like Keifer. But lord knows I need him right now. "Thank you," I whisper and then fall into his chest. "Thank you, thank you, thank you."

"You and Keifer need couple's counseling."

I adjust my grip on my pool cue. "I think you mean family counseling."

Oliver burps. Gross. "Whatever. You know what I mean."

I take my shot and knock one of the remaining pool balls into the pocket.

"Good shot."

"Thanks."

Piper's having a playdate, so I invited Oliver out to a happy hour for beers and pool. Keifer was not so conspicuously left out of the plans. Oliver didn't push back, though. This has become a new norm. He's had to take his role as the middle child to the next level by being the go-between.

I grab my beer. It's gotten warm from my hand, but I don't care. I drink down the murky remains of the beer and watch Oliver set up his shot.

"How long do you think this is going to go on, though?" He takes his shot.

I shrug. "Until he's not mad at me."

"Or until you apologize."

I shake my head and round the table, looking for a clear shot. "Keifer told me explicitly to stay away from–"

"Oh, bullshit. Come on, what is this? Grade school? You and June are adults. You just need to make an apology and then we can all get over it. Things are weird enough with Rowan and Trevor..."

I find a good clean shot and start to position my cue. "You think they're done?"

"Not done done... but close to it." Oliver shakes his head. I know it's been weighing on him, the crumbling of his best friend's relationship. "Anyway. We need some semblance of normalcy."

I swallow. If only it were that easy. I start to bob my cue back and forth, ready to hit the ball. Oliver grabs my cue and pulls it up.

"What the fuck, man!" I stand and come face to face with my brother.

Oliver's the tallest of all of us, but he's really as sweet as a puppy. And the look in his eyes isn't threatening at all. It's determined. "You're a man, aren't you?"

I raise my eyebrows.

"Because a man apologizes when they've fucked up, Jarred." Oliver pushes me aside and sets his cue where I just had it. "And you, man? You fucked up." He takes the shot, the pool balls racking together wildly.

Little does he know how much I really fucked up. How deep this goes. How awful the things I've done are.

But he's right. A man apologizes. Maybe I'm not a man at all.

"That was my shot, doofus."

Oliver snorts. "Whatever."

"Big yawn!"

Rye smiles, the bags under her eyes not outshining her happiness. "Yes, indeed. Very sleepy."

"Probably drank too much milk," Dad says teasingly from his spot in his easy chair. On his paternity leave, he's taken on a completely different persona of a guy who wears only sweatpants and T-shirts. Makes me imagine what things were like when I was just born with him and Mom. Was he so relaxed and at ease? Or was he tremblingly terrified?

Piper giggles. She's cuddled up to Rye's side, staring down at baby Ivy. She's gotten much more comfortable around the baby and often asks about her. But when it's not "when can I see Ivy?" it's "when can I see June?"

I sometimes think the same thing. When can I see June again? Never, if Keifer has his way.

It's our third visit to Dad's house since Ivy's birth. We let them get settled the first week, didn't want to get in their way. Now, we're always around. That way I can help out where things need it, and Piper can get quality time with her grandparents and the new baby.

"Daddy, can we get a baby?"

We all laugh. "Maybe someday, kiddo. Some other things have to get in order before then, though."

"Like I'd need a mommy," she says matter-of-factly.

I purse my lips and nod. "Probably a good start."

"What about June? June would be a good mommy!"

I freeze.

"And you like June! And I like June!"

Luckily, Rye and Dad don't seem to suspect anything. Rye speaks first. "You're right, Pipes. June would make a good mommy. But June will probably start a family of her own one day."

Piper frowns. "But you became Daddy's mommy."

Rye, Dad, and I all exchange looks. *Ew. Weird.* "It's a little different, kiddo."

"A lot different," Dad follows up.

We laugh again. Things were awkward at first, being the same age and all, but we've figured it out. Once my brothers and I saw how happy she made Dad, we didn't question their relationship at all.

Piper screws her face together. "Something stinks."

Rye sniffs the air. "Uh-oh. Someone needs a change, don't they?"

Ivy squalls in response, extending her little hands toward Rye's face. Leave it to the baby to redirect the conversation.

Dad gets up from his chair. "I got her." He retrieves Ivy from Rye, rocking his hands back and forth to take the tiny baby into his arms. "Jarred, come with me."

I scoff. "You need help with a diaper change, Dad?"

"No, I want company. Come on." I can tell by the look in his eyes he has something to say to me. What it is, I can only hazard a guess at.

I glance at Rye and Piper. Rye smiles. "Go ahead. We're good here." She wraps her arms around Piper: cuddles are bliss for my daughter.

I get up and follow Dad out of the room and up the stairs to Ivy's nursery. He lays Ivy down on the changing table, cooing to her lovingly. "You're a stinky girl, aren't you? We're going to get you cleaned up."

I'm a dad. I know all the weird things you say to your kids. But watching my dad say them is really fucking cringy.

I take a seat in the rocker across the room and start to rock back and forth. "Oh, this is nice."

Dad glances back at me. "State of the art rocker, naturally."

"Naturally. So, what's up?"

"Well," Dad says as he cleans Ivy. "I noticed your discomfort at the 'mommy' conversation."

I laugh. "Yeah, I mean, you would have felt that way too."

"I know. I was lucky that you boys were grown when your mother passed away."

We were teens when Mom died in the car accident. We were able to conceptualize and understand. It was rare any of us mentioned Dad's ongoing bachelorhood after she was gone.

"But Piper's so young. And you're so young, Jarred. You're in your twenties still."

"Nearly thirty, you mean. Over-the-hill."

Dad glares at me and I laugh. "You know what I mean. A lot of people your age have never been married, let alone have children."

"What's your point, Dad?"

"I just think–" He steps on the pedal of the garbage can and tosses in the dirty diaper. "It's time you get out there."

Aw, fuck. "Dad, this isn't the time. Things at work are tense and–"

"Things aren't tense. You're tense. You know, I didn't say anything after the whole June thing, but where did that even come from, you know?" Ivy blathers and Dad leans down to kiss her nose. "Yes, where did that come from, sweet girl?"

I roll my eyes. "I don't know, Dad."

"You need to relax."

"So, you're saying I need to get laid."

Dad puts his hands over Ivy's ears. "Tender ears, Jarred."

"Well, that's what you're saying, isn't it? That I need to relax and–"

"No. That's not what I'm saying." Dad pulls her onesie back on and tucks Ivy into his shoulder. She's impressively tiny compared to him. "If you found someone to share your life with for Piper's sake... for *your* sake... you'd be happier, Jarred."

My mouth gets hot. "You're not suggesting that *June*—"

"No, of course not." He bounces Ivy a little back and forth. This man is a master at multitasking. "But putting yourself out there to find someone... I think it'd be really good for you."

"It's not just a switch I can flip."

"I know, son."

"You know, women aren't pounding down my door."

"Not *yet*." He gives me a lopsided smile.

"That's a lot of work. And time that I don't have. I don't have the time to get hurt again."

Dad sighs. "Don't let Meredith run your life, kiddo. She may not be here, but you sure are letting her control you."

My chest tightens. I think he's right. I've been operating under this fear of abandonment, of pain, even when it's not justified. I'm still letting her take my happiness.

Dad licks his lower lip. His eyes fall to the ground. "Just think about it. Okay? You can't live your whole life believing you don't deserve a second chance." He glances at little Ivy who is gurgling at his shoulder. "Trust me. I know a thing or two about that."

He leaves the room, but I don't move a muscle. If I'm

honest with myself, I'd love someone to share my life with. To share Piper's life with. She deserves it... maybe I do, too.

My mind goes to June. She's the closest thing I've had to that since Meredith. I've tried to pretend like I can play it cool, but I should have known my feelings would get the better of me. I'm too smart to just discard something like that.

I need to talk to her. I need to get this out. Maybe she can forgive me. And we can be friends. Maybe more. God, I pray more. Because my heart opened to her in just those two weeks. It welcomed her in and adored her every way that I could. I pretended it was just physical. But it wasn't. I was falling in love with her. I know that now.

If she doesn't want me, that's okay too. I can deal with a broken heart. But I need to clear my conscience. Otherwise, I will be trapped by the weight of my affair with Juniper Reed forever.

A cold fear spreads through my veins.

I have to get through Keifer first.

And that might possibly kill me.

23

JUNE

Keifer and I have met up at a coffee shop near my house. A quiet place where we can talk and know that no one will be trying to listen. I haven't seen him since he took me to the hospital. He was adamant he'd support me, but he also needed time to process the truth of my pregnancy. I can't blame him. If the tables were turned, I'm sure I'd feel the same way.

It's given me several days to sit with the information and decide what I'm going to do. The first day, I was pretty sure I was going to get rid of it. I don't even have a job; how could I possibly think I'm in a place to have a baby?

But the longer I sat with the idea... with the feeling... the more I realized how much I wanted it. I want to be a mother. I want to have a baby.

Most of all, I don't want to be alone anymore. And as much as I don't want to think about Jarred, this baby is his. A piece of him that I want to keep with me forever.

Keifer approaches the table with our coffees. He's wearing his office best. It's the middle of his workday and he told me he couldn't wait until it was over to speak with me. "Espresso shot for me... decaf black for you..."

I smile. "Thank you." I've been taking the job of expectant mother seriously. I've already thrown out all the junk food and alcohol and started taking prenatal vitamins. Decaf coffee is just another thing on that list. Although I have to say, without the caffeine, I'm exhausted.

"Um, I take it that you're keeping the baby, then."

"You're well-read on the dos and don'ts of pregnancy, huh?"

Keifer flushes. "Not really. You know how much Rye complained about having to drink decaf. Just picked up on it."

I wrap my hands around the steaming cup of coffee. "Yes. I'm going to keep it."

Keifer smiles sadly. "Is it weird to say I'm glad?"

My eyes prick with tears. I've been so quick to cry since I've found out the news. I'm not sure if it's the pregnancy hormones or me *thinking* it's the hormones. "It's not weird at all."

"Okay, good. I just... I'm pissed off, June. I'm still mad about everything."

"I understand."

"Especially that you didn't tell me. That you thought you could just sweep it under the rug. I never thought we'd hide anything from each other."

I take a sip of coffee. It scalds my tongue. "I didn't know what to say, Keifer. You can understand it's not the easiest thing in the world to talk about."

He nods. "Trust me, I've seen it from your perspective. I know it must have been hard. But I have to value my feelings first. And it hurt, June. It *still* hurts."

I stare into the steam curling up from my coffee mug. "I'm sorry, Keifer. I never wanted to hurt you."

Keifer doesn't reply. He drinks down his espresso in one gulp and then clears his throat. "I'm going to respect your wishes to not tell Jarred. I don't blame you after how he's treated you. That's not the Jarred I thought I knew."

I lower my gaze. Me either.

"That's your journey. Not mine." He raises his eyes to mine, an intensity to his gaze that I've rarely seen in him. "But the baby should have the Hawthorn name. So I'm willing to be the father on paper."

My heart leaps with an unexpected joy. "Are you sure?"

"I wouldn't say it if I wasn't."

I bat away my tears. "Thank you. Thank you, you don't' know how much that means to me."

Keifer's expression softens. "Of course, I do." He reaches across the table and squeezes my hand. "June, you're my best friend. But that doesn't truly cover it. You are a sister to me. I would do most anything for you. You know that, right?"

I nod. "I just don't know what I did to deserve it."

"Stop that. You know what you've done. We have twenty years to show for it." Keifer squeezes my hand. "You need to let me support you. At least a little. If you need a job, we can hook you up with something at Hawthorn. But I'm not going to let you struggle, especially with a baby on the way."

I wrap my other hand around our interlaced grip. It's wrong that I've assumed I was alone this whole time. I wasn't letting Keifer in. I cut him off. That's why I've felt so alone.

"And I better be the godfather."

I laugh. "Of course. Of *course*. But that means you need

to get a nicer apartment because if something happens to me, my baby will not be raised in a pigsty."

"It's not a pigsty!"

"*Keif...*"

He rolls his eyes. "Anyway. You just have to promise me. No more secrets. I don't keep anything from you, you don't keep anything from me. Deal?"

"Deal."

"Good." He glances at his watch. "Shit. Gotta head back to the office. You okay if I leave you here?"

"I'm good. Thank you for coming up to meet with me."

"Anything for you, June."

We both get up and embrace. The brother I never had. The brother I've always had. He kisses the side of my head tenderly and then heads out, waving at me over his shoulder.

I sit back down and sip my now tepid coffee. My baby will be a Hawthorn. I hadn't even thought of that, but the idea that my baby will be a Hawthorn is euphoric. My baby will get to be something I've always wanted for myself (as much as I don't want to admit it).

I touch my stomach that still feels the way it always has. I can't wait for the moment I can tell the difference, the small swell and firmness that will indicate, yes, there really is a baby here, growing. "Baby Hawthorn... how do you like that?" I whisper. I've already started talking to it. How could I not? This baby is my partner in crime. I know it's selfish to want a baby so I'm not lonely. But I know I'll give this kid the best life possible. I have a heart so pent up with love, it's ready to burst. I will shower him or her with all the affection, love, and attention I can muster.

And together, we'll be unstoppable. My little one and me.

24

JARRED

I stand at the door of Keifer's apartment. I've been here so many times, but I've never felt full of terror like I do now.

"Keifer, I need to tell you something," I mutter to myself. "Keifer, there's something you should know." I've practiced a speech so many times, but I can't seem to lock it in. It never sounds right. I know he's going to be furious with me no matter which way I go about it. Might as well just get it over with. I raise my hand and knock. Silence.

"I'm sorry." The words feel funny. "I'm sorry. I'm sorry, sorry, sorr—"

Suddenly, the door flies open and two hands wrap around the lapels of my jacket. I'm pulled into the apartment and slammed up against the wall with so much force that my head hits the wall and puts stars in my eyes.

"You've got a lot of fucking nerve."

Through the stars, I can see the face of Keifer. My little brother. He's furious, like a caged animal finally freed and ready to eat its captor. *Jesus Christ.*

"What the hell, Keif?" I cry out. I grab him by the wrists and struggle with him until I'm able to gain the upper hand

and throw him against the opposite wall. "What the fuck is your problem?"

Wrong thing to say. A moment later, his fist connects with my jaw. Uppercut. A good one if I weren't on the receiving end. Pain blasts up from my chin through the rest of my face and I rocket back to the wall behind me. "Fuck!" I shout. "This isn't a fair fight!"

"You think you deserve fair?! When you use June up and then treat her like dirt?!"

His voice rings in my ears. "What?"

Keifer shoves me away from him. "She told me. About Michigan. About everything that happened between you two. What the fuck, man? How could you do that to her?"

I rub my jaw. It's tender, but nothing's broken. "Let me explain."

"Explain what? You fucked her and then you decided because she opened her legs to you, she didn't deserve your respect. Isn't that right?"

Is that how she feels? Is that what she's saying? "That's not how I feel at all. *At all*, Keif."

"Could have fooled me."

Oh my god. I've hurt June. Perhaps beyond repair. I can't see straight. Whether that's because of the blow to my head or because my thoughts are spinning anxiously, I can't be sure. "I promise, I never did anything to hurt her on purpose, I promise."

"I wonder if she even wanted it. How am I to know if you didn't force her into something she didn't want to do?"

Is the story I'm telling myself that far from the truth? "Is that what she said?"

"No, but given the way you've acted, I don't feel like I even know you anymore. How do I know you aren't capable of something like that?"

That's the thing that pushes me over the edge. I start to cry, sliding down the wall slowly at the thought that I'm some sort of monster. "What have I done? Oh god, what have I–"

"Stop it. This isn't your pity party. It's not going to work on me."

I don't have the words to reply. I weep into my knees, my whole body shaking. I don't recognize myself anymore. I've let coldness infiltrate my life when I should have been running toward warmth. Toward June's sunlight.

"Are... are you seriously crying? Is this real?"

I nod heavily, hiccupping through tears, "Y-yes."

"Oh my god. Oh shit." Keifer kneels down and touches my shoulder. "Did I hurt you that bad?" He touches the back of my head where a lump has started to form.

I wince. "That's not w-why I'm c-crying."

Keifer frowns at me.

He already knows the truth. Now it's up to me to give him my side. No holding back.

"I haven't been able to stop thinking about June since we were at the cabin," I croak. My tears start to abate. "We agreed we wouldn't bring things back to Chicago. For the family's sake. But I... I think I love her, man."

Keifer's eyebrows jump. "Seriously?"

"Seriously. She's warm and bubbly and fucking gorgeous. I have so much fun with her. And the way she is with Piper..." My heart leaps into my throat and a few more tears escape my eyes. "That did it for me. Piper loves June, and I can see it. I can really see June taking care of Piper and being in her life and being the mother figure. If she wanted to be. I don't know. I don't know anything anymore."

Kiefer rubs my arm gently. "That's a lot, man."

"I know. It's so much." I lean my head back. "It's a lot."

"Yeah, you just said you want June to be Piper's mother. That's..."

I swallow. It's painful from all the tension in the front of my throat. "I do."

"And that you love her."

"I do."

"It was just two weeks, Jare."

I look at him and smile limply. "Maybe. But hasn't it really been twenty years?"

Keifer sits down and rests his arms on his knees. "Damn, when you put it like that..."

We are quiet for what feels like a long time but can't be more than a minute. The reality sinks in. Not only do I love June, but I've told someone about it. Despite the pain in my jaw, it feels amazing to tell someone the truth.

"I had no idea you were hurting so much."

I shrug. "It's okay. How could you know?"

"I just thought you were being a jerk."

"I can be. I was. It just wasn't from nowhere. I was trying to protect myself. But I never wanted to hurt June. Never in a million years would I want to hurt her."

Keifer's lips twist to the side. "Well, you have."

I sigh. "I know. Clearly."

"So, with Piper there, were you guys like... affectionate in front of her?"

I shake my head. "No, not physically. But I doubt she didn't pick up on something."

"That explains why she's asking about her so much. I can't believe you've been able to keep her quiet."

"Had to buy her silence in the form of toys."

"Smart girl." Keifer looks away. "You know, June's my best friend."

I close my eyes in resignation. "Trust me, I know. That's why we tried to move on from it. We didn't want to hurt you."

"Well, you should have just told me. Because I can't imagine a better guy for June than one of my brothers. And between you and Oliver, you aren't as much of an idiot. *Most of the time.*"

I smile. "Yeah. Most of the time. That's... that's really nice to hear."

"I'll help you get her back."

Relief floods through my body. "Really?"

Keifer nods.

"That means the world to me. It really does."

His expression is extremely serious. "But If you ever hurt her again, I'm choosing her."

I swallow. "I understand."

"And I'll tell everyone about how much of a jerk you were to her."

"That's fair."

Keifer spits on his hand and holds it out to me. "Shake on it."

"Do we really have to do the spitting thing? We're grown-ups."

He narrows his eyes. He won't accept any less.

"Fine..." I spit on my hand and shake his hand.

Keifer beams at me. "Good. Now let me get you some ice for your head. Then we can get down to business."

25
<hr>

JUNE

I read the text from Keifer with a smile on my face. He's taken to endearingly calling me "mama," and every time it makes me giddy.

I could use a break from the job search anyway. And he's right, a little fresh air will do me good, especially now that I'm starting to spend more time hung over the toilet in the morning. It can be miserable but my little one is worth it.

"What do you think, honey? Want to go see Uncle Keifer?" I talk to the baby a lot even though it's still so early on in my pregnancy and the baby hasn't developed their hearing yet. I can't help it. I already feel like we're best friends.

I reply to the text affirmatively and head in the direction of Belmont Harbor almost immediately. I wonder what Keifer has planned. He's been taking such good care of me since we found out about the baby. I don't know what I did to deserve a friend who is so forgiving and attentive like him, especially after my betrayal of his trust, but damn, am I grateful.

Keifer's car is already in the lot, so I pull into the spot next to his. When I step out of the car, I hear him call out for me from the park that separates the cars and the lakefront. "Hey! Over here!"

I rush over to him. "Hey! What's up?"

"I have a surprise for you."

"What kind of surprise?"

Keifer smiles mischievously and doesn't reply. We walk together for only a few steps before I spot a picnic blanket topped with a basket. I can't help but smile. "Did you do all this for me?"

He shrugs and picks up another blanket from the setting. "You'll need this. Here." Keifer throws the blanket around my shoulders. "Should warm you up."

"Thank you."

Keifer glances over his shoulder at the parking lot. "Um. I forgot something in my car. You wait here. Make yourself comfortable. There's lots of food in the basket and a thermos of tea too."

"I'll wait for you to come back to crack it open."

He nods and then hurries back toward the parking lot. I sit on the blanket and take in all the scenery. The park by the harbor is mostly empty. After all, Chicago is still trying to shake that winter feeling. But there are people taking walks and biking along the lakefront.

The water is beautiful blue green, still trying to thaw from the winter.

Blue green. Just like Jarred's eyes.

His image floods into my mind despite my wishes. I lift my head to the sky, basking in the warmth of the sunlight.

The dissonance of the warmth and the cold combined with the image of Jarred's eyes brings me right back to the cabin.

God, I miss Jarred and Piper. I miss what the three of us had so much.

I close my eyes and am transported back in time to that little pocket of time where we all belonged to each other. I have a memory of the three of us sitting outside on the deck, bundled up so tightly in our winter clothes. Sitting around the fire pit, roasting marshmallows.

Piper was sitting on my lap, holding her skewer with a marshmallow on the end. She kept putting them too far into the fire and charring them to bits, which made her laugh more than anything. Eventually, though, I had to guide her through the perfect way to roast a marshmallow.

"Not too deep in the fire... yeah, right there... now, you see how it's browning?"

Piper's eyes were very focused. "Uh-huh."

"You're doing it perfectly, Pipes. You'll be a pro in no time."

We pulled the skewer out of the fire and Jarred swooped in with a graham cracker and chocolate all ready to go. "Okay, s'more time."

When we were around Piper, we were careful not to be too obvious that something was happening between us. It would have been so easy for her to take just a little kiss or a touch and run so far into fantasy with it. We wouldn't have been able to recover.

How foolish we were to think we could ever recover.

But anyway, the memory. Jarred fixed up her s'more and Piper took a big bite, chocolate and stick marshmallow all over her mouth. "Mmm. Good."

We all laughed.

Jarred squeezed in beside me on the lounge chair and

put his hand next to my hip. Not around it, next to. He traced his thumb up and down the firmness of my jeans as he watched Piper eating her s'more while she sat on my lap.

There we were, the three of us. Like a little family. Not *like* a family. Really a family. We just didn't know it then. But I know we both felt it. That palpable energy connecting us in that instant.

God, that memory. Makes me so happy and so sad at once. I wish I could have more of those memories with Piper and Jarred. Especially now, knowing about the life inside of me. We all have so much love to give each other.

But it can never be. I'll have to nurse that heartbreak the rest of my life.

26

JARRED

Keifer rushes over to meet me at my car. "She's all yours, man."

I embrace him tightly. "Thank you."

Keifer pats my back. "Take care of her."

"You know I will. You know it."

He smiles at me and then lets me go.

Into the unknown.

I start to walk toward the park and spot June almost immediately. The sight of her takes my breath away. Her auburn hair is down, being tousled by the breeze. She holds her face up to the sky, showing off her elegant profile as she basks in the sun.

As I get closer, I see her eyes are closed. And a tear is running down her face. But she's smiling. What's she thinking about?

When I get to the blanket, she still hasn't noticed my approach. I kneel down and tenderly swipe the tear from her cheek. "No more of that, huh?"

June opens her eyes wide at the sound of my voice and

the touch of my hand. Hazel and dark brown, drawing me in like a spell. I withdraw my hand from her even though I want nothing more than to pull her into my chest and hold her and kiss her. "What are you doing here?"

I take a deep breath. "I had Keifer help me set this up. I knew if you'd known it was me, you probably wouldn't want to see me. But I need an opportunity to apologize to you. After everything that's happened between us, the way I've acted is absolutely inexcusable. Even if things hadn't... well, it was so wrong of me. And I need you to know, June... Juniper. I'm incredibly sorry. So, so sorry. And I'll do anything I can to make it up to you."

Though I wouldn't blame June if she was furious with me, a smile appears on her lips. "Thank you, Jarred. That means a lot to me."

I smile and nearly laugh in relief. "Good. Good. I'll apologize a million more times if you like, but—"

"No, I don't need that." She pauses and then opens the picnic basket. "Just share a meal with me, will you?"

My heart flutters. "Gladly."

We start to break open the picnic basket. There are fresh berries, cheese and a baguette, piping hot tea, veggies and hummus, small tea cakes... it's a perfect spread.

Things are awkward at first. Both of us are clearly trying to be as kind and careful as we can, not wanting to break our newfound space of forgiveness. But it's clear we're both trying. It starts with pleasantries: "How've you been?" and "How's work?" and it's not long before we're able to transition to our former rapport.

June makes me smile and laugh more easily than anyone I've ever met. I don't know how I didn't know this sooner, after knowing her for so many years. But I'll take every moment I can now.

"How's Piper?" she asks eventually.

"She's... she's good."

June doesn't reply, reaching for a handful of black-berries.

"She misses you."

She stops. Her eyes are unable to meet mine. "I miss her too."

"I feel like I took you away from her. Like I stripped her of some joy."

June shakes her head. "You were just protecting your-self. Protecting her. You can't blame yourself for doing what you thought was right for her."

"How could it be right when all I did was hurt you? Right in front of her?"

"Jarred, please don't be so hard on yourself. We were trying to cope. I think we probably both thought we would be able to move on from what happened when in reality..."

The way she trails off gives me hope that I've been on her mind too. "I missed you, June."

Her lips perk up in a sweet but sad smile. "I missed you too."

"You made me really happy when we were together. You made Piper happy. And that's everything to me. You know that." I feel my lower lip trembling. Fuck.

"I'm glad. I wasn't sure, after everything. It seemed like I hurt you by being around." Her voice has gotten so small it breaks my heart.

I have to choose all my words carefully. "It hurt to be around you because I knew I still wanted what we had at the cabin. Still *want* what we had."

June moves closer to me. Her hand hesitates in reaching for mine. She puts it on her lap. "Why didn't you tell me? Why didn't you say anything?"

"Because I was terrified."

"Of course, you were terrified. So?"

"'So?!'"

June giggles. "You know what I mean. That's life. That's... feeling something for someone."

I want to come right out and tell her I love her. But it feels like too much too soon for both of us. That's not why I wanted a moment alone with her anyway. Hopefully, that will come with time. "The last time I felt that way for someone, I got burned, June. I got burned really bad."

Her brow folds, gently coaxing me to say more.

"I was so young when I met Meredith. And you know, my parents were incredibly young when they met and had me and got married. Too young. I know that now. I felt this pressure to find someone as soon as possible. So when I met Meredith, I couldn't help but love her. All of the things that should have been red flags or that should have given me pause, I ignored." I lower my eyes to my lap. "Because I was determined to love her."

A breeze whips around us and we have to take a moment to make sure things don't blow away before I continue. "But my dad and brothers knew it wasn't a good match. I ignored them."

"I never knew Meredith well. I thought you two were very much in love when I saw you."

"She did a good job of fooling you, then." I laugh sadly. "That was her gambit, you see? She just wanted my money. Didn't love me beyond that. At least that's what I've come to understand now after all the time I've spent with lawyers arguing about alimony."

June grabs my hand. The shock of her touch is so great I think I might burst with happiness. "I had no idea."

"Right, of course. I don't tend to talk about it. Because it's so embarrassing."

"You shouldn't feel that way, Jarred. You opened your heart to someone. That's a beautiful thing. And you have Piper... that's a *beautiful* thing."

"Yes, Piper..." My little girl. I wouldn't trade her for the world. But her origins sometimes break my heart. "Meredith didn't want kids. But I wanted to be a father so bad. So, she gave me that. But she treated it like a sacrifice. Her body, her career, all of these things. From the moment Piper was born, Meredith resented her."

I have to stop for a moment. It's hard to talk about. I try to ignore the impact Meredith has had on my life, but it's impossible when she is directly responsible for the greatest gift in my life. One I know has lots of questions about why her mother has chosen a life without her.

June shifts even closer to me and wraps my hand in both of hers. She holds it to her chest. "You don't have to talk about it."

I swallow back my sadness. "No. I want to. I have to. You deserve to know." I raise my gaze to hers and feel a charge of confidence from her. "She left so soon after Piper was born that I felt responsible. That I had made her have a baby, coerced her, manipulated her. But no. She agreed so she could hold Piper's custody over my head and squeeze more and more money out of me."

"That must be so scary."

"It used to be. Now I understand that I never really knew who she was. She was just a person I created in my mind. Meredith was never perfect for me. I made her up to be that way." I squeeze June's hand back. "You can see, now, how it's hard for me to trust myself when I feel attracted to someone or–" I stop myself. *Don't say love.* "I can't do that to myself again. And I can't do that to Piper."

June nods. "Of course. But you've never had to protect yourself from me, Jarred. You know that, don't you?"

I touch her cheek softly, remember that tear running down her face. "I know that now. I'm sorry I didn't trust your kindness. Your beauty."

She flushes around her nose. God, she's adorable.

"Can you forgive me?"

Her lips curl up; she's going to say "no", I just know it. There's a pain in her eyes, something she hasn't said out loud. I've ruined everything. I deserve her distance.

"Of course, I can," June finally says.

"Thank you."

"And I know it's not about that, but I'm not sure if I can ever go back to what we were. What we had."

That breaks my heart the slightest bit despite knowing she's right. "I understand. We'll start as friends. And there's no pressure for anything to happen between us again. I mean that."

June smiles. Her warmth pours from her skin. She glows in a way I never knew she could. I want to tell her how beautiful she looks. I hold my tongue.

"Would you be open to seeing Piper? Spending a little time with her?" I can't help but keep her close. And Piper is as good an excuse as any.

"I'd like nothing more, Jarred."

"Good. Good. Could I have your number?"

She laughs. "All these years and you don't have my number?"

I look away sheepishly. "Guess I took it for granted that you'd always be there."

June tilts her head to the side and shakes her head. "That's just the thing, Jarred. I *will* always be there."

My fear melts. June's not like Meredith. She's true to her word. She's a good person. And she makes my world a better place.

And for better or worse, I will wait for her until she's ready. Even if it's the rest of my life.

27

JUNE

Jarred is trying really hard. It's honestly adorable.

He sends me a text good morning, a text goodnight, a complaint about his day, a picture of Piper, a funny meme, something that makes him think of me.

He's trying *really hard.*

And I feel awful that I can't seem to manifest that same energy. I'm terrified that he'll hurt me again. And with his baby on the way, I don't want him to get too close only for him to pull away again. I have to be very careful.

Today, though, I'm going over to his place for the afternoon to see Piper. She's been looking forward to it all week. At least that's what he told me via text last night.

I'm getting ready now, trying to look like I've tried, but not *so* hard that it makes him think I'm trying too hard. Ugh. It's complicated.

I swipe a clear lip gloss across my lips and fluff my hair as I look in the mirror. I've taken a liking to my reflection since becoming pregnant. The hormones are already starting to clear up my skin imperfections.

Hopefully, he doesn't suspect anything.

My phone dings and I pick it up. Unsurprisingly, a text from Jarred.

> Someone's excited...

He's sent me a picture of Piper sitting at the front window looking at the street. Already waiting for my arrival even though I'm not supposed to be there for another half hour. I grin and text back.

> Can't wait to give her a big hug and kiss!

Three dots appear.

> If I tell her that, she'll start running to your house. Best to save the surprise.

I smile and start to put the phone down when another text comes through.

> I'm excited to see you too.

My smile fades. Why does that scare me? Just a few weeks ago, there wasn't anything I wanted more than Jarred to give me a sign that something was still between us.

Now that it's real, it feels much more complicated.

I heart the message, unwilling to type the words back to him, and focus on getting ready faster. I've got a little girl to see ASAP.

———

I barely make it out of my car before Piper is bounding out of the house. I can't believe it, but she looks bigger, even feels bigger when she leaps into my arms.

"Junie! I've missed you!"

The sound of her voice fills my eyes with tears. Fucking hormones. "You have no idea how much I've missed you too, little one." I rock her in my arms for a long moment. I can't wait for this with my own baby. Will it feel as full? Will my baby hold me as tight? I hope so.

Jarred appears in the front door of the townhouse. I try not to stare at him over Piper's shoulder, but he's a fucking sight to be seen. He's wearing a simple white button down with the cuffs rolled up to his elbows and slacks that hug his package just enough that my imagination starts to run wild.

Not now, June.

"Come on, Piper, let's let her get inside first."

I put Piper down, but she stays right at my side while I grab a gift bag out of the passenger seat.

"Is that for me?!" she asks eagerly.

"You bet it is. Let's go inside and you can open it."

I walk up the stairs, Piper's hand in mine, and meet Jarred.

"You really didn't have to bring a gift, June," he says in a low voice.

"I saw it and immediately thought 'Piper'. I had to get it for her."

He smiles at me. I can't believe it, after the scowls and indifference that he still has that sweet, private smile for me.

"It can be an early birthday present, Daddy," Piper reasons, pulling me into the living room.

I gasp. "That's right! Your birthday is coming up! I can't believe you're turning ten!"

Piper laughs loudly. "Not *ten*! Four!" She shows me

four raised fingers of her right hand, as if I need a visual to understand the amount. So cute.

We all go to sit down. I set the bag down in front of Piper. It's teaming with colorful tissue paper. "I hope you like it."

"I will!" she announces. She pulls every sheet of tissue paper out of the bag, throwing them over her shoulder like confetti.

"You're making a mess, Piper," Jarred chides light-heartedly.

Piper ignores him and pulls out the gift: a furry stuffed kangaroo. I don't know what it was that made me think of her. Maybe it's my hormones overacting, but when I saw it, tears flooded my eyes. I knew I had to get it for her.

"It's a kangaroo!"

"It *is* a Kangaroo." I grin. "Open her pouch."

Piper pulls open the flap of fabric at the kangaroo's belly and pulls out a little baby kangaroo to match. "It's a baby!"

"Well, look at that," Jarred remarks softly. I glance over at him. He's smiling, leaning his elbows on his knees, watching.

Being around him again fills me with a feeling of safety and comfort I haven't had in a long time.

"What do you say, Piper?"

Piper looks to me, green eyes shining bright. "Thank you, I love them!" She rushes over and hugs me, her new kangaroo between us. I squeeze her back, pressing a kiss to the crown of her head.

Aw fuck. I'm crying. Just a little. A couple crystallized tears. I can swipe them away quickly unless–

"June, you're crying," Piper remarks, touching my arm softly.

I shake my head, but my tears betray me. "It's nothing.

It's because I'm happy." And hormonal. "I'm so happy to see you."

"And Daddy," Piper says.

I swallow and glance to Jarred. Blue-green eyes. A piece of heaven. Could it be mine again? Was it really mine ever? "Of course. And Daddy."

Jarred looks away, flushing, a lock of blond hair falling to his eyes. It's slightly perverse for me to call him "Daddy". I don't mean it any differently from the way Piper says it. But watching him blush makes my mind go there for the briefest moment.

I want his touch again. Want his whole self.

I want Jarred to give me everything he has. In order to get that, though, I need to be willing to give him my whole self too, and I'm not quite there yet. I still have to work through the fear he'll abandon me again. And I can't have that, especially when I'm carrying his baby.

"Can we play?" Piper asks, pulling on my hand.

"*After* dinner, Pipes," Jarred instructs as he gets to his feet. "Come on. Food's already on the table."

"Fine, but I'm bringing Franny."

Jarred and I exchange a glance of bewilderment.

"Franny?" I ask.

"My kangaroo! I'm calling her Franny."

Jarred and I both laugh.

"That's a great name for a kangaroo, I think. What's the name of her joey?"

"Frankie."

"Brilliant," Jarred says.

Piper leaps up and rushes through the doorway into the dining room. "Come on, Franny and Frankie! We need to find your seat!"

Jarred and I are left alone in the living room. I glance over at the tissue paper. "I should clean that up."

"No, I'll get it after dinner."

"Oh, it's no trouble."

"June. You're the guest. You don't have to clean up after anyone."

I stop. My life from now on is going to be a lot of cleaning up. After my baby. *Our* baby.

Jarred comes toward me. My heart races. Is he about to kiss me? He can't. Not yet. We aren't ready. I can't even look at Jarred without my heart bursting open, without desperately wanting to pull him into my arms and tell him how close we already are.

"You really didn't have to bring her a gift."

"I wanted to. I've missed her."

I wait for his response, but before he can, Piper cries out from the dining room, "Hey you guys! It's dinnertime! Come on!"

I can't help but laugh. "Coming!" I turn back to Jarred. "You heard the lady."

He looks as if he's been interrupted, his mouth slightly ajar and eyes flicking back and forth across my face. He shakes it off, though, and smiles. "Can't keep her waiting, can we?"

Children... always make things complicated. And Piper is a living, breathing one. One who is healthy and happy. I can't imagine what kind of complication it would be to tell Jarred about the one yet to come into the world.

That's a secret I'll have to keep. For how long, though... I'm no longer clear.

28

JARRED

It's wrong. It's so wrong. But I woke up hard and I have to do something about it. It won't go away no matter how much I try to go back to sleep.

I wrap my hand around my length and try to concentrate on release. A didactic and objective sort of thing. Nothing erotic, nothing specific.

However, June is never far away from my brain. She hasn't been since January. This isn't the first time I've thought about her while touching myself. Won't be the last.

I've imagined her in so many scenarios: fucking her in her bed at the cabin, fucking her in my bed here, fucking her in the shower, having her suck me off under my desk, but the more I've thought about her while masturbating, the more nuanced the fantasies become.

Today, I'm imagining walking into the kitchen while she's washing the dishes. Her beautiful, apple-shaped ass in a pair of jeans.

I bury my head in the pillow and grunt as I pick up the pace of my strokes.

I go up behind her and take her by the hips softly, rub

my hardness against her. She'll laugh and glance up at me with her glimmering, mismatched eyes.

"*Fuck...*"

Just the thought of grinding up against her has my head swimming. I've got it so bad for this girl. So fucking bad it's embarrassing.

I can hear her voice, whispering, as if she's right in my ear. *Something you like?*

Every time I think about kissing her, my cock jumps, and this moment is no different. Too excited at the thought of June's plush lips on mine and my hips grinding against hers.

And then, a thought comes out of nowhere. One that I've never had about her. At least not consciously.

I want to put a baby in you.

Where the hell did that come from? Doesn't matter. It gets me going even harder. I start fucking my own hand. The thought of... breeding her. Of truly making her mine.

God, it's making me hornier than ever.

My imagination stutters, picture shifting. Her naked body comes into focus behind my closed eyelids. Our bodies connected as I thrust inside her.

Her ragged moan thrums through my brain. *Come inside me.*

I want to come inside her so bad. I want to spill my seed into her and watch her grow with my baby. Fuck, fuck, *fuck.*

Suddenly, I'm hit with orgasm, my eyes shooting open and my mouth gasping for air dryly.

"Holy shit... holy shit..."

Jacking off has never felt this good.

I can only imagine how the real thing would feel.

I collapse back into the pillows with a heavy sigh, my

bare chest heaving with shame. June and I are so far from that point that it's embarrassing I've even thought about it.

Since our meeting at the park, she's come to see Piper three times already. These were all at my invitation. In fact, every conversation we have over text is initiated by me. I can't blame her. But every time my phone vibrates, I pray it's June. I just want to know she's thinking about me.

Because I'm obviously thinking about her. A terrifying amount. I don't know if I'll ever be able to stop.

I clean myself up and fall back asleep for a while. It's the weekend so I have a bit of time before Piper's up.

I'm awoken by my phone buzzing with a notification. Probably one of my brothers or my dad.

I reach over to the nightstand limply and pull my phone off the charger.

June.

It can't be. I wipe the sleep out of the corners of my eyes and blink them a few times.

There it is. Right on the text message notification. Four perfect letters. *June.*

I can't open the notification fast enough. I have no chill when it comes to her. I'm not playing any games, no waiting around to reply so I can look like I'm a cool guy with other stuff on my mind. I open the text. It's a chunky little paragraph. My heart leaps into my throat. *Oh god,* I'm already expecting the worst. What if she tells me this isn't working? She doesn't want to talk to me? What if she's found someone else?

I just have to read the damn thing.

Good morning :)

Well, that's a good sign.

I want to thank you for inviting me to see Piper so much. You have no idea how much it means to me right now. If you'd like, I'd be happy to sit for her if you're ever busy. Only if you're comfortable with it, though.

I find myself typing before I register my thoughts.

Absolutely. She'd love that. I would too.

I wait for the three dots to appear and just when I'm about to put my phone away, they do.

Good. That makes me happy.

Hearing that June is happy makes *me* happy. I've got it bad for this woman. I feel like a freshman with a crush on the captain of the cheerleading team. I haven't felt this way about someone since...well. Since ever.

My phone buzzes again. A double text? This must be my lucky fucking day.

Also saw this and thought of you. RIP our snowman ;)

It's a meme with a melting snowman. I don't even read it, can't even read it. She sent me a meme! That's the equivalent of an "I love you" this day and age, isn't it?

Jesus Christ, calm down, Jarred. You're taking things slow, remember?

We continue texting for a little bit and land on a time for June to take care of Piper this upcoming week. I know she hasn't gotten a new job yet. She must be struggling. I try to offer to pay her, but she refuses.

Later, when I tell Piper that she and June are going to have a playdate later that week, she's excited beyond belief and leaps into my lap, bestowing wet kisses to my face.

I contemplate sending a text to June later in the day to let her know that Franny and Frankie, the kangaroo pair, are never far from Piper's side, but I stop myself.

Why am I beating around the bush? I know what I want. For me, for my daughter...

I want June. And I want to stop pretending I can live without her.

I can't.

And I need to tell her.

29

———

JUNE

Free for dinner tomorrow night? 7pm?

I stare at the text and feel my heart leap into my mouth.

Is this a date? Is Jarred asking me on a date? I need clari-fication.

Sure, I can come over then.

Three dots. Waiting, waiting. Amidst the waiting, the microwave goes off. I forgot I put in a mug of hot water to make some tea.

No, just me and you. We'll go out somewhere.

I abandon the tea in the microwave and start to pace around the first floor of my house. This feels like he's asking me on a date. But I don't want to assume and make a fool of myself. I already feel like I've done that too much with Jarred.

Like a date?

No three dots. No response. I stare at my phone until it hurts my eyes and then toss it on the couch. I don't stop pacing. I run through the events of the past few weeks in my head. Last time I saw Jarred was when he came home while I was babysitting Piper. It was an awkward conversation mostly because I was feeling extremely nauseous and didn't know how to explain it away. Whoever called it "morning sickness" clearly was underestimating that it can be an "all the time" kind of sickness. And at three months along, I'm feeling it big time.

Sooner or later, it's going to be impossible to hide.

My phone buzzes and I lunge to grab it. He's texted back.

Yes, like a date, June :)

A moment. Then another text.

Is that okay?

I'm torn. On one hand, I'm ecstatic and want to start jumping up and down. This is everything I wanted almost from the beginning. Not just a relationship kept hidden from the light of day, but something more. Much more.

I think I love him. I *know* I love him.

And yet, on the other hand, I'm full of dread.

I don't yet know if I trust Jarred. And everything in my life is so tender right now, from my breasts to my emotions. If I were to be hurt again, it wouldn't just be my emotions and my life on the line.

It would be our baby's.

I can't trust myself. I don't know if I'm protecting my feeling or self-sabotaging.

Someone else needs to make this decision for me.

———

"I don't understand the issue." Keifer rushed over as soon as I called him, and I can tell he thinks I've pulled him away from work for something trivial. "Do you want to go out with Jarred or not?"

"It's not that simple, Keifer."

"Actually, June, it really *is* that simple," he replies and kicks his feet up on the couch. His suit is starting to rumple. "If you like him, you go on a date with him. If you don't, you don't."

I'm still pacing. Haven't stopped since the text came through. "You know it's not that simple."

He frowns.

I point at my belly. "*Helloooo.*"

Keifer rolls his eyes. "Okay, fine. A minor complication."

"You have a weird definition of minor."

"It's his baby, June. This could be a great steppingstone to–"

"It's not about the complication of him knowing about the baby or not. It's–it's–" I stop and take a deep breath. "I can't have him cast me aside again. I wouldn't be able to handle that. Especially not now. It would break my heart. Completely and utterly."

Keifer's expression softens. "Aw, June. He's not going to cast you aside."

"You don't know that."

He laughs wryly. "Okay."

"Don't 'okay' me."

"You're moody today."

"I'm *pregnant*, Keifer!"

"I know! Yeesh!"

We both go silent. I cross my arms over my chest and stew for a long moment.

"June, you can only act on behalf of your own emotions. How do you feel?"

Jesus, when did he become so wise? "I'm terrified."

"That's not what I mean. How do you feel about Jarred? What would you want in a perfect world where you knew you couldn't get hurt?"

I look down at the coffee table and focus on a water stain from a cup. I'm scared to say it. It's taking everything in me to force the words out of my mouth, but I finally blurt, "I love him. I want to be with him."

Keifer doesn't reply. I look at him. He's smiling.

"Don't look at me like that."

"June's in *looooove*."

"Stop! Stop it! You're making it worse!" I cover my ears. With Keifer, I always feel like I'm nine and cooties are still a thing.

"If that's how you feel, you have to go. You know that, right?"

I nod. "Yeah. You're right."

"Plus, Jarred hasn't asked anyone on a date in... since before he was married. This is a really big deal. He wouldn't do that if he wasn't taking it seriously. *Really* seriously. And you know he takes everything seriously with Piper around."

My lips perk up at the sound of Piper's name. I might not know Jarred as well as I would like quite yet, but I do know one thing. Piper is at the front of his life. He wouldn't be asking me out if he wasn't serious.

Keifer sneaks up on me while I'm dazed in thought and snatches my phone out of my hand. "Great, I'll send the text."

I chase Keifer around while he unlocks my phone (I really need to change my passcode from my birthday) and types out a message to Jarred.

More than. Can't wa

Keifer sends the text early while I'm tugging the phone out of his hand. "Keifer! 'Can't wa'? Seriously?"

"Your fault!"

I glare at him while I retype the message.

*can't wait. Sorry. Got too excited.

Jarred responds immediately.

I can't wa either. ;)

I smile to myself and put the phone to my chest.

"Aww... You *love him*."

I elbow Keifer in the ribs, but my smile doesn't fade. I can't believe it. I'm going on a real date with Jarred Hawthorn.

———

I tentatively walk into the restaurant. A French bistro downtown. When I looked at the menu online, my wallet cried.

The restaurant is eerily quiet. It doesn't even look like any patrons are here which is strange for a Friday night in

Chicago.

The hostess greets me with an easy smile. "Are you Juniper Reed?"

I take a deep breath. "I am."

"I can take your coat."

I hand over my coat, the skin of my neckline pricking with chill. She gestures deeper into the restaurant. "Your table is straight back. You won't miss it."

I thank her and walk further into the restaurant. It's beautiful, like taking a step into a piece of Paris.

But as soon as I see Jarred, the rest of the world pales in comparison to his beauty.

He's standing beside a table set for two in the middle of the restaurant, adorned with beautiful flowers and lit candles. His hair is perfectly tousled, his navy suit tailored perfectly to show off his lean body.

And his blue-green eyes sparkle at the sight of me. "Wow. Hi."

I giggle. "Hi."

We are both quiet, the gap between us getting smaller as I approach the table. I stop a foot in front of him. Should we hug? Shake hands?

"You look amazing."

I blush and glance down at my dress. It's my signature little black dress I've had for years. It still fits like a glove and shows off all my curves. Luckily, my tummy isn't one of those yet. "Thank you. So do you."

Jarred touches my arm. "May I?"

I nod, unable to speak.

Jarred kisses my cheek softly, but the feeling of his lips lights a fire in me. "Thank you for joining me tonight."

"Thank you for inviting me."

As soon as Jarred leaves my orbit, my heart sags. I want him close like that always.

But first. Dinner.

Jarred is a perfect gentleman, pulling out my chair for me and then circling to his own.

"It's very quiet for a Friday night."

He chuckles as he sits. "It better be. That's what I paid for."

My eyebrows jump. "You... rented out the whole restaurant?"

Jarred smiles. "I wanted to be alone with you. Is that alright?"

"Yes, but... that's so much."

He shakes his head. "Nothing's too much for you, June. Believe me." Our eyes meet. "You deserve it."

I can't even speak. Jarred is making such an effort to make me feel adored and cared for. It's going to be impossible not to fall deeper into my love for him. Not that I want to resist...

Jarred reaches for a bottle of red wine on the table. "Tell me about your day."

He starts to move the bottle toward my glass, but I cover it with my hand. "N-none for me!"

Jarred cocks an eyebrow.

"I'm..." Fuck, got to come up with a good lie fast. "I'm not going to drink tonight. It's not good for my nerves."

"Oh, June, you don't have to be nervous around me."

I blush. It's only half a lie. Even if I wasn't pregnant, it'd be better not to drink. "It's a good nervous. I promise."

Jarred hesitates and then puts the bottle down.

"You can drink! I don't want to stop you from having fun."

He shakes his head. "No, you're right. I want to be as

clear-headed as possible for tonight. Take everything in." His eyes glimmer. "Take *you* in."

From there, conversation flows as easily as the wine would. We banter, laugh, even bring up memories from our time at the cabin. Not the ones from the bedroom, but still, intimate ones. Cutting up snowflakes, making pancakes, sledding. We talk about Piper and how she's doing in school, how Rye and Ash are doing with the new baby (god, I've missed so much), and what is happening at the company. When conversation turns to me, I try not to linger. I don't have much to tell. No new job, no interesting events or travels. Just a baby on the way.

The longer we sit there and reminisce, the more I want to tell him. But I don't know how. It could ruin everything. I can picture his laughter dissipating and smile fading. Any possibility of a future together could disappear.

No, the moment has to be right. Extremely right.

———

"It's a nice night."

We're taking a walk down the lakefront path. The lake is calm tonight, sloshing gently against the retaining wall. Jarred and I walk side by side, our arms occasionally brushing.

After dinner, he asked if I wanted to continue our night together. Of course, I said yes. Even without the lubricant of alcohol, it feels so easy. I could spend the whole night with him. And the whole of tomorrow. And every tomorrow after that.

"It is," I say quietly.

My hand brushes his accidentally. I recoil as if he's burned me.

Jarred glances over at me and smiles bashfully. "Sorry. I'll keep them in my pocket."

He starts to slide his hands into the pockets of his light jacket, but I stop him, catching his hand in mine. My heart's beating fast as all hell. And I'm just holding the guy's hand. I'm totally screwed.

Jarred gasps softly but doesn't draw away. Doesn't let go.

"Is this okay?" I ask.

His smile tells me enough. We continue to walk hand in hand past Oak Street beach and all the way down to the North Avenue overpass where a car is waiting for us. By that point, his arm is around my waist. I wonder if he can sense a change in my body. I barely can, I doubt he could. But if he remembers my body like I hope he does... maybe.

Jarred directs the driver to take us to my place. I feel a disappointment creep into my bones. The night is coming to an end. I don't want to be patient for something to grow. Something already has bloomed between Jarred and me. I need to know now if I can trust it.

The car pulls up to my house in Mayfair. Jarred follows me out to walk me to the front door.

"Sorry for keeping you out so late," Jarred says as I fish for my keys in my purse.

"You should get back to Piper, huh?" I ask.

"No, no. She's staying with Keifer.

"At his place?!"

Jarred laughs. "No, I'd never! They're at my house. I told him not to wait up."

"Oh."

Alarm breaks out in Jarred's expression. "Not that I assumed anything would–"

I giggle. He's totally out of sorts at the implication.

"Or that you would even want to, you know, spend more time with me than we already–"

"Jarred."

His motormouth stops.

"Do you want to come inside?"

Wide-eyed, he nods. "Y-yeah. I'd like that."

"Me too."

We stare at each other for a moment. Feels like we might kiss. But Jarred abruptly backs away. "I'll go tell the driver to head out."

"Sounds good."

He's back in a flash before I can even unlock the door fully. It's adorable how he's tripping over himself. We head inside and I direct him to sit on the couch. I offer him a glass of wine which he accepts. I'll pour myself one too, but I won't drink it.

"It's the only bottle I have in house. Hope it's not bad," I preface as I hand him a glass.

Jarred's eyes shine like the moon. No one's ever looked at me the way he does. "I'm sure it will be fine. I won't even taste it, to be honest."

We sit there in silence for a moment. He takes a sip of the wine, mutters, "Good," and takes another.

I chew on my lower lip. It's awkward. Not in a bad way. "So, I've had a nice time tonight."

"Me too," Jarred replies.

We look into each other's eyes. My heart is pulling on the back of my tongue. *Don't say anything that can hurt you. Don't let him hurt me.* I can't live my life hiding from the love I feel, regardless of what it does to my heart if it's not reciprocated.

"What are you thinking?" Jarred asks.

I swallow. "I'm scared."

His brow tenses. "Why, June?"

"Because I like you a lot."

He smiles. "I like you a lot too. Some might say *like like*."

I can't help but laugh, even though there's still an undercurrent of ache. "I don't want to get hurt."

"I'm not going to hurt you, I promise. Not again. I'm sorry I ever did in the first place."

I shake my head. "It's not that simple."

"Believe me, I wouldn't have invited you out if–"

"It's not you. It's me. It's all my shit that I have going on that isn't letting me trust you and I need to trust you if anything is going to happen between us. And I don't know how to–" My voice breaks. I don't want to cry in front of him. But the weight of the past four months is so great. I feel like I'm starting to break under the pressure.

"Hey, hey, hey..." Jarred reaches out and touches my cheek. "Talk to me, June. Tell me what's not letting you trust me. Maybe I can help."

His touch makes me want to fall right into his arms and never leave. How can my body trust him when my brain doesn't? "I don't want to bother you."

"Are you kidding? You're not a bother. I want to be here for you. I'm *trying* to be here for you. You can tell me anything. Anything at all. I promise." His voice is earnest. He isn't leaning away.

It all comes pouring out.

"For so long I've believed I'm meant to be alone. And I don't mind it sometimes. I like my space. I like to do my own thing. But... you know, I've never had a big family. I just had my parents. And when they moved away, they didn't even ask me how I felt. They just made the decision, closed on the house in Hilton Head and then gave me notice." I thought I'd come to terms with this pain, but it smarts just the same as it always has. "So, I've learned to be alone."

"June, I'm sorry. I never knew that it was so... out of your control."

I look down into my lap. Shame is starting to close in around me. "I've never had a boyfriend more than six months. Everyone always finds a reason that I'm not good enough to stick around for."

Jarred leans closer to me, hand wrapped around the nape of my neck so he can make sure I look him in the eye. "That has everything to do with them, not with you, June. I mean, look at me. I was so caught up in all the promises we'd made and everyone else that I ended up hurting you. That had nothing to do with you. Nothing."

There's one thing I don't want to say but I know I have to. To make him understand. "I lost my job because the dad was hitting on me."

The air leaves the room. I haven't said this to anyone. Not even Keifer. In some ways, I think I've told myself I deserved it.

Jarred's touch loosens on me. My insides beg him not to go. "What?"

"He started hitting on me a couple months before I was fired. And I always sort of laughed it off as like sexist humor... I didn't want to take it too seriously or else I'd have to deal with it. But he started doing it more and more and–"

"How did *you* lose your job when he was–"

"His wife caught him commenting on my... on my body." I can remember where I was standing in their kitchen. I was wearing yoga pants and he wouldn't stop staring at my ass. *"When are you going to let me take a bite out of you?"* he asked. And that's when his wife walked in. Before I could reply and refuse. "She blamed me for provoking him with my clothes. And implied I had been trying to seduce him for months."

I feel myself suffocating. "I promise, I wasn't. Not at all."

"Of course, you weren't. You don't have to defend yourself to me."

Now that the truth is out, I can't help from spilling everything. "She called me a whore and threw me out on the spot. Not even a goodbye to the kids." I touch my belly without thinking and quickly draw it away. I don't think he noticed.

Jarred is silent. His jaw tenses and releases. "I'll fucking kill him."

"Jarred–"

He launches himself up off the couch and starts to pace furiously. "I'll kick both their asses. And they'd deserve it. How dare they do that to you?"

I lower my head, tears running down my cheeks. He's right. How dare they?

"After all the work you did for them. The love you gave their kids. I know you, June. Juniper." Jarred comes back to me and puts his hands on my shoulder. "You do everything with so much love. And anyone who abuses that... They don't deserve you."

"But that's the thing! Everyone abuses it, Jarred! Everyone. Even my own Mom and Dad. Why do I even try anymore?" I sob.

"Look at me."

I do. Our eyes lock.

"I won't. I know I've done it before. But I won't ever again. Believe me, June. I want to protect your love with everything I have in me." He wraps my face in his hands, wiping my tears away. "Trust me."

I want to give into him so badly.

I think I will.

Jarred pulls me into his chest and I collapse, weeping on his shoulder. I fit so perfectly into his embrace. I can't believe I've been resisting.

"Please trust me," he whispers.

"I do."

In an instant, our lips find each other's in a firm kiss. Jarred's lips feel just as nice as I remember. Exhilaration runs through me, and my tears abate. When we draw away from each other, a smile crosses his lips. "What?"

"I've wanted to do that for a long time."

"Me too."

"Since the moment I left the cabin, I wanted to run right back to you and kiss you." Jarred kisses me again. "To hold you." Again. "To tell you how much I want you. Not just your body... your everything."

I run my hands down the lapels of his jacket, feeling the contours of his chest beneath his clothes. "Why not both?"

Jarred's pupils dilate.

I get up off the couch, his hand in mine. "Follow me."

He doesn't speak, simply follows the pull of my hand up the stairs and into my bedroom. We tumble onto the bed in a frenzy of laughter and arousal. But this time, not a single thing about this is wrong. The feeling doesn't have to be hidden the moment it's over.

Jarred stills. "Are you sure you want to do this?"

"We don't have to if you don't–"

"No, I just don't want to rush you." He cups my cheek in his hand, thumb gracing the corner of my lips. "I want to do this right."

I smile and get up onto my knees. "Then take off my dress."

Jarred laughs. How can he resist a temptation like that? He pulls my dress up over my head and then caresses the curves of my waist. "Fuck... no wonder I've been dreaming about you."

In no time flat, we are both naked, kissing and touching.

Jarred's fingers delve between my lower lips, his thumb skimming my clit. I've been more sensitive since I've been pregnant. If he touches me too much, I might just come. "So wet, baby..."

"I want you inside. Don't make me wait. Don't make me beg."

"I won't. I promise."

Jarred positions himself between my legs, tenderly cradling me underneath him. But before he slides inside me, his eyes meet mine. "Juniper Reed, I..."

I buck my hips up to meet his.

"I've got you."

Jarred slides inside. He feels the best he's ever felt inside me. With each thrust of his hips, I feel electricity thrumming through my stomach, through my heart, to my throat. I am unrepentantly vocal about how good he's making me feel.

We don't exchange many words. Our bodies are doing enough. And my emotions are out of control. Tears well into my eyes.

"Are you alright?"

I nod. "Feels... so good. Keep going."

Jarred wraps his hands around my hips and quickens his pace. I moan loudly and wrap my arms around him tightly, burying my face in the crook of his neck.

"Oh god, June."

I'm shaking.

"*Juniper...*"

I capture his lips in mine as a tremendous groan comes out of me and my body rollicks into orgasm. Jarred is no more than a second behind. His teeth gnash on my lower lip as his hips stutter inside me, releasing every last bit he's stored up in the past three months.

Little does he know, he's already done the trick in that regard.

We both try to catch our breath. Jarred raises himself up to his elbow and strokes my arm with the backs of his fingers. "Was that alright?"

"What do *you* think?"

He chuckles. "I never want to assume."

I run my fingers back through the skeins of his blond hair. His eyes flutter shut. This man could be mine forever if I play my cards right. And there's nothing I'd like more.

"Better than alright. The best, Jarred. The best."

And, in my head, just for me, I say it.

I love you.

30

JARRED

June. In my arms. In her bed. Her body tangled up with mine just as I remembered. Better than. Her hand is plastered to my ribs, feeling my breath as my chest rises and falls. I run my hand through her long auburn hair and kiss her forehead. She nestles in closer with a contented sigh.

The moon is streaming in through her bedroom window, casting a pale, silver glow across her bare body. She's magical. Perfection. I adore her.

"June."

"Hm?"

I draw back to look into her eyes. Even in the dark, they're striking.

"I love you." It comes out easily. Unfettered. That's how I know it's right.

Her breath catches, her lips part in wonder at the notion.

"I know it's a lot. It might sound like too much. And I hope I don't sound crazy when I say it." I touch her cheek. "But Juniper, I've loved you since the moment we left the cabin. Before that even. I feel like I was always meant to love you. You filled my life with joy and sunshine for that short time and I've just been trying to get back to you. Does that make sense?" I sound off my rocker. "It probably doesn't. Shit, I probably sound like– "

"I need to tell you something." Her voice is light and tremulous. Something's wrong.

"Okay. Anything. You can tell me anything."

June retreats from me, sitting up and glancing out the window. Preparing herself. I'm already prepared for my heart to break, to shatter into a million pieces. She sits up, still bathed in moonlight. I even love her when I'm afraid she's going to destroy me. "Jarred, I'm pregnant."

My brain either freezes or melts. I'm not sure which. Pregnant? It's just a bunch of letters. I can't conceptualize the meaning.

"It's yours. If you thought I might have... I don't know." June takes a deep breath. "And I'm keeping it. I wasn't going to tell you. I didn't want to be a burden."

Never. She'd never be a burden.

"I don't know if this changes your love for me."

It doesn't.

"But I love you. I love you so much."

Why can't I get my mouth to express the thoughts in my head?

"I know this is probably a lot to digest, so... I've given it some thought and there are a few options. The first being you don't have to be a part of my life or the baby's life. I wouldn't hold that against you. It's my choice to have it, so if you're not interested, I can't blame you."

My god, the way June has had to suffer knowing this and wondering how I might react when I found out.

"Or you could be part of the baby's life. You wouldn't owe me anything. Your love or your time. You could just be a dad. You're such a good dad and I'd be so grateful for our baby to have you in their life." She stops and sucks her lower lip into her mouth. As if those are the only two options.

What about letting me be a part of her life? We love each other. We've both said that.

The present moment suspends. I remember the only other time I've been here before. When Meredith told me she was pregnant with Piper. I was younger then. Twenty-four. Terrified to be a father, but excited. Beyond excited.

But Meredith...

I remember her face when she handed me the pregnancy test. She had turned almost gray. And her eyes. More terror than joy. Dread.

"I don't know what to do," she had whispered, crossing her arms over her chest.

"Nothing, Mer. You're perfect. You're already perfect." I wrapped my arms around her. We both cried. I thought we were on the same page. I desperately believed that even when she grimaced at her changing body in the mirror and pushed me away when I tried to touch her.

I thought then that all she needed was some encouragement. I thought I could love her into loving our baby.

That clearly didn't work. And when I could see it wasn't working, I poured all that love into Piper. That's when Meredith finally left. That's why I'm here now.

June, on the other hand, has already made a choice much harder than Meredith had to make. She was prepared to go at this alone. To become the mother to my child without me.

I return to this moment, the one in June's bed, drowning in moonlight and the weight of admission after admission.

I can finally focus on her face. She's blinking back tears.

I don't want her to cry again. No more tears, not on my account. "Or...?" I ask.

"Or we do this together," she says, lips perking in a tentative smile. "We build a life together. With Piper. With our baby." June tucks her hands against her stomach tenderly. The baby is already a part of her. A glorious, beautiful part.

This is how it's supposed to feel. Mutual joy. Mutual fear.

Love.

I reach out and take her hand. "June, I would want nothing more."

Full of relief, June returns to me, falls into my chest. I draw her up into my arms and kiss her. The first kiss after we've both admitted to loving each other and wanting to be together. The first kiss now that I know she's having my baby. Her lips have never felt so perfect on mine.

June pulls back and looks up at me with adoration. I slide my hand down to her waist and slide my thumb back and forth across her skin. "You really want to do this. With me?"

June nods and presses my hand to her belly. "I've never wanted anything more."

I beam at her. "I need you with me all the time, June."

"I know."

"No, I mean it. Literally."

She lets out a tinkling laugh. "What do you mean?"

"I need you with me. With Piper. I want you to move in with me as soon as possible."

June's eyes go wide. "Are you serious?"

"Of course. We need to start our life together as soon as possible. We need time to get our family in order before our baby–" Those two words leave me breathless. "Our baby, June. We're having a baby together."

She grins. "We are."

I wrap her face in my hands, looking into her beautiful eyes. I've gotten so lost in them before. But now, I don't feel lost. I feel like she's found me. "Thank you."

"Don't cry, honey."

I can't help the tears welling up in my eyes. "You'll never know the huge honor that it is to be told a woman wants to have a baby with you." I sniffle and breathe steadily to keep myself from crying. "I want to be able to take care of you."

"Okay."

"I don't want to wait."

"You don't have to."

"I want to make up for all this time we've wasted. The months. The *years*, really."

"We have lots of time to make up for it, Jarred. Lots of time."

I kiss her forehead. "No one can get in our way."

"Well, if you're worried about Keifer, don't be. He knows I'm totally in love with you."

I gape. "He knows I'm totally in love with you!"

We both laugh and fall back into the bed, snuggling under the covers, talking about everything we've been dying to talk about in our time apart. We go through everyone's reactions and try to gauge how they'll feel. We talk on and on about Piper, how we'll tell her, muse about how happy she'll be. Eventually, it's later than late and June is nodding off in my arms. I'm still wide awake, though, going through every possibility for our future. I can't keep my hands off her stomach. It'll go faster than we want it to. Soon, we'll be able to know the gender and she'll start to feel the baby moving. She'll get bigger. We'll have to pick out names. Decorate the nursery. My brain is spinning.

As if I've been saying my thoughts out loud, June sleepily touches my chin and kisses my cheek. "We have all the time in the world, Jarred."

That's all the reassurance I need to get me to fall into dreamland with her.

31

———

JUNE

"June! Put that down!"

I stop halfway up the walk to Jarred's front door–or should I say *our* front door – and spin around. Ash comes barreling toward me and swipes the box I was carrying out of my hands. "Ash! It's just a box of clothes! Relax!"

"I don't want you carrying anything. Not right now. Alright?" He says to me over his shoulder as he heads into the house.

I stand in the middle of the walkway with a resigned smile. It's the first weekend in May and the weather is *perfect*. Warm enough that I'm only wearing a cardigan. I glance back to the U-Haul parked on the street.

Keifer, Oliver, and Jarred are all arguing over who's going to take what. "I can't carry the books! I've got a back issue!" Oliver exclaims.

"You're too young for a back issue," Keifer says.

"I can help," I call out to them.

They all turn; each of them wears the same look of incredulity. If they didn't have similar features already, that would be all the proof you'd need to tell they're related.

"Or not…" I trail off, shaking my head.

The guys all grab a box and start walking down the path single file, the rear taken up by Jarred. He stops in front of me. "I told you not to lift a finger…"

I splay my hands out and twiddle my digits. "Oops."

"You're impossible."

"I can carry *something*. I'm not an invalid."

"*June.*"

"Come on… I don't want everyone to treat me like I'm some porcelain doll."

"Honey, there are four of us. You genuinely don't have to do anything. Besides…" He props the box up on his hip and touches my waist. Nearly four months pregnant and I'm just starting to show. Since it's my first baby, it takes a bit longer. Even though it's not visible to most, Jarred and I have eagerly noticed and celebrated the change. "You're doing plenty of heavy lifting already."

I snort and push his shoulder. "You're a cornball."

Jarred blushes. "Please just take it easy?"

I touch his chest. "Fine…"

"Thank you." He leans down and gives me a soft kiss on the lips.

Keifer groans as he and Oliver come out to grab another box. "Gross, guys."

"Sorry, Keif," Jarred says, but he's grinning. Clearly not sorry.

"Oooh… Jarred and Juniper sitting in a tree–" Oliver starts to taunt.

Jarred rolls his eyes. "Seriously?"

I laugh. "I'm surprised this hasn't happened sooner."

"K-i-s-s-i-n-g."

Jarred pushes past his brothers to take his box inside, leaving the taunt in his wake.

"First comes love, then comes–well, you guys fucked up the whole rhyme," Oliver says cheekily.

I can't help but smile. I think I've been smiling for two weeks straight since Jarred and I confessed our love to each other. It all happened so fast. The very next day, we told Piper and then the day after that, at family dinner, Piper told everyone else. She walked right in the door and said, "Daddy and June are in love and they're having a baby!"

Now *that* was a record scratch moment.

Of course, the announcement required many explanations. Explaining a relationship was one thing, but a relationship and a baby? Woof. That was a lot. But with Jarred and Piper at my side, I wasn't worried for a second. Jarred and I took turns explaining the situation. Even Keifer added in his perspective. Once he gave his blessing, everyone seemed to relax.

"This kind of thing runs in the family," Oliver had said with a look to Rye and Dad. He received a jab in the ribs from Keifer for that one.

"I was waiting for one of my boys to come to their senses and date you," Ash had said, pulling me into a big hug.

"I'd say welcome to the family, but that'd be redundant," was Rye's response as she rocked baby Ivy. "Since you've been a part of this family longer than me."

Jarred had put his hand on the nape of my neck at that moment, sensing my overwhelming emotion. Why did I spend so much time questioning it? They'd been my family all along.

Since then, Jarred and I (and Piper) haven't been apart. We've decided to keep the house in Mayfair for the time being and continue to rent it out as secondary income. I've been able to give up my job search and focus solely on Piper and nesting for the baby. I have to admit, being a stay-at-home mom sounds like the perfect thing for me. Not loving another family but loving my very own.

I can't wait.

While the Hawthorn boys shuffle boxes from the truck and back, I go out to the backyard where Piper is playing with Franny and Frankie.

"What are you doing, Pipes?" I ask as I sit down in the grass across from her.

She stares at the stuffed kangaroos and then looks at me. "This is like you and the baby, right?"

I nod. "It's very similar, isn't it? I just don't have a pouch."

Piper laughs. "That'd be silly."

"Silly, but convenient!"

Her laughter dies down and is replaced with a thoughtful expression, considering her stuffies. "I'm not your baby because I wasn't in your pouch."

I furrow my brow. "That's not how it works, Piper."

She looks up at me with wide, crystalline green eyes. "But, June, you're not my real mommy."

"Well, you're right. I didn't carry you in my pouch, like you said." I pull her into my lap and hold her close to me, brushing her hair out of her face. "But I love you just as much as if I had."

Piper's lips twist. "Really?"

"Mhm."

"But what about the baby? Don't you love them more because they're your *actual* baby?"

I've had a lot of practice loving children who aren't my own. I've never loved any as much as Piper. Perhaps because she is an extension of Jarred, it makes it so easy. "You are my actual baby, Piper. I don't love you any differently than the one I'm having now."

Piper smiles bashfully and tucks her head against my chest. I kiss the top of her head and rock her. Two weeks. That's all it has taken for us to form this intense bond. There are going to be ups and downs, no doubt. That comes with the territory when you're raising children. But in the deepest part of my soul, I know Piper is mine. I don't care what any birth certificate says.

It doesn't take much longer for the boys to bring everything inside. There isn't much that I really needed to bring from the old house, but the front hall is crowded with brown moving boxes.

We repay the guys for their work with pizza and beer. We all sit outside on the deck in the twilight, sharing a meal together. Piper and I sip on lemonade. She insists on sitting on my lap and while Jarred is being overly conscientious of my pregnancy, a little girl on my lap isn't going to be too much.

"Shouldn't you be running back to Rye and Ivy, Pops?" Keifer asks with a mouthful of pizza.

"Trust me, she's happy to get a moment away from me. I think she's feeling a bit smothered by my attention."

"Perhaps it's time to end your paternity leave?"

Ash shakes his head. "Are you kidding? And miss all the firsts?"

"Yeah, you don't want to miss any of those," Jarred concurs.

"First smile, first time they lift their head..."

Jarred nods excitedly. "First time they start talking back!"

Oliver groans. "We get it! You guys are dads!"

I touch Jarred's hand under the table. Our fingers dance together softly. He glances over at me and smiles. We'll get to share all those firsts together soon.

"No, your mother was the same way," Ash says wistfully. "Mothers need time alone with their babies."

Piper shimmies in my lap. I can't tell if she's really listening, but I pull her tighter into me in case she's thinking about her mother again.

"So, June, now that you're all moved in, you're going to have to come hang out at my place," Keifer says.

"What? Why would I subject myself to that?"

The table laughs.

"So I can talk about my brothers behind their back! Don't tell me you're going to run and tell on me to Jarred whenever I say something bad about him!"

My friendship with Keifer is still a work in progress. We're still getting used to the Jarred factor. Now, a lot of my time is taken up by being with Jarred and Piper and more still will be dedicated to the baby. A conflict of interest in a sense. It's why Jarred and I avoided each other in the first place.

However, I know he's happy for us. He became each of our confidants as we were trying to find our ways to each other. Without him, this wouldn't have been possible.

"June, I give you permission to not tell me what Keifer says about me behind my back," Jarred says, squeezing my hand.

"Now *that* is the height of romance," Oliver announces.

I smile at Keifer. He rolls his eyes but smiles anyway. We'll get through it. Jarred and I have already discussed asking him to be the godfather. We haven't mentioned it to him yet, but I don't see any other possible option. After all, he already stepped up to be the baby's father once. I know he'd do it in a heartbeat if he had to. Now if only he'd hurry up and find a wife in the next five months so that we have a godmother to match.

I glance down at Piper. She's nestled into my shoulder and soundly sleeping. It's been quite a day for her. I rub her back. "I think it's time to wrap things up."

———

Later, much later, in the room that now belongs to both Jarred and me, we are bathed in a post-coital glow. Not only are we making up for lost time, but my hormones are on another fucking level. Jarred is doing his best to keep up with my sexual appetite.

"I don't think I can go again tonight," he sighs into my chest, his lips grazing the inside of my breast.

I run my fingers through his hair. "S'alright. I'm exhausted anyway."

Jarred lifts his head and narrows his eyes. "Are you feeling alright?"

"Yes, honey. Just tired."

"Mm. I love when you call me honey." He trails kisses down my sternum to my stomach where he rests, gently stroking the nearly imperceptible swell.

"You know, Piper's getting worried that I'll love the baby more than her."

Jarred sighs. "Well, that was inevitable."

I nod sadly. "Do you think we rushed her into this?"

He smiles. "Are you asking if I think we rushed Piper into knowing that you'd be around to love her forever? No."

That's all the reassurance I need.

"It was going to be difficult no matter what. Her life's been more difficult than she deserves."

I touch Jarred's cheek. His eyes flutter shut. "She has a great life, Jarred. You've done everything in your control to do that for her."

"I think out of everything I've done to give her a better life, you're the best."

"I'm the best thing you've *done*?" I scoff.

Jarred laughs, blushing. "You know what I mean! It sounded better in my head."

I pull him up to lie next to me, nestling into his embrace that has become so familiar. "I know what you meant, honey."

Silence. The best kind. Full of love. Nothing hidden.

"Juniper?"

Warmth floods through my body.

Jarred's hand widens against the plane of my belly. "Welcome home."

EPILOGUE
JARRED

"Don't panic."

"I'm panicking."

"Jarred. Breathe."

I take a deep breath as Dad suggests. He puts his hand on my back as I do so. His touch is steadying.

"It's going to be fine."

I widen my eyes. "Fine?"

He sighs. "Great. It's going to be great."

I nod. I've been planning this night for two months already. Only a month after June had moved in was I sure. I want her to be my wife. I don't want any question of what we are to each other.

After work one day, I went to buy her a ring, determined to ask right when I got home. But when I saw her beautiful smiling face and her burgeoning belly, I knew she deserved much, much more than just a spur of the moment proposal.

She deserves perfection.

Oliver rushes into the front hall to meet Dad and me. "Jarred! Keifer just texted. They're almost here."

"Oh my god." I start to feel a little bit faint.

"Whoa, buddy. Nope." Dad claps his hand on my shoulder. "You're good."

"I just did this before and it wasn't good, it wasn't good at all. What if this isn't good? What if it's–"

Oliver grabs my other shoulder. "Jarred. June isn't Meredith. You know her, man. You do."

"Right. You're right." I didn't have this vote of confidence from my family the last time. In fact, I didn't even tell them until after I had done it. I tried to ignore how crestfallen my dad looked when he told me congratulations. If he's standing here encouraging me, that's all I need. I adjust my suit jacket. "Everyone's outside?"

"They're all there."

"And Piper? She's ready to go?"

"Yep. She's adorable. It's going to be perfect."

I hear a car door slam as clear as a bell, shooting my gaze over to the front door. It's happening. Now or never.

And never isn't an option.

Dad and Oliver give me a few more words of encouragement, but they sound like they're underwater. My thoughts are too loud.

Don't panic... It's going to be perfect... She's going to love it...

I open the front door and am immediately hit with August warmth. Fall is already in the air, cutting through the sweltering Summer heat.

Keifer's car is parked close to the front walk. He's helping June step out from the passenger seat. And oh my god... She's stunning. She wears a loose lavender dress made out of a silky looking fabric that accentuates the curve of her belly so perfectly and a pair of fashionable white tennis shoes. Seven months pregnant. I have a hard time keeping my hands off of her when she's not pregnant, but when she is, I'm completely glued to her.

June and Keifer are laughing about something when I finally get the courage to greet them. "Hey guys!"

They turn to look at me. June's eyes brighten. She's spent so much time in the sun that her shoulders are freckling. In all the years I've known her, I never noticed that. "Hi, honey."

"Sounds like you two had fun." I go over to her and kiss her temple, wrapping my arm around her waist. "You three, I guess."

"You should have seen how much popcorn June was able to put down. It was *insane*." Keifer crackles.

"Hey! It's not my fault." She runs her hands over the mountain of her stomach. "He's a growing boy!"

Yes, we've known we are having a boy from the moment we were able to find out. We have our little girl, Piper, and now she'll have a baby brother. How perfect is that?

"And you're very sensitive!" Keifer retorts.

"You better run!" June holds up her hand and tries to playfully bat him on the arm, but Keifer dodges it.

"Missed me!" he says and backs away into the house. As he does so, his eyes meet mine. My last vote of encouragement.

June sighs. "He's so annoying."

"Tell me about it. He's my little brother."

She grins and touches my suit jacket. "Why do you look so nice?"

"I could ask the same of you. You look... amazing."

"You told me to dress up. Although I've never known family dinner to be a formal affair."

"Well, today's a little different."

"Oh? How come?"

She's so sweet and pure and not suspecting this at all. Last we spoke about marriage, June thought we needed to wait longer. "Don't get me wrong, I'd marry you in a heartbeat. But this is already so crazy. Wouldn't getting engaged be even crazier?"

Short answer: yes. Long answer: yes, but I don't care.

"You'll see. How are you feeling, hm?"

"Back is killing me."

"Aw, poor thing." I kiss her forehead. "You want me to give you a back rub."

"More than anything, but I'm afraid if Keifer catches you behind me, he'll think you're trying to stick it in."

I chuckle. "Well, I usually am."

"Jarred, you're so bad." She takes my hand and rests it on curve of her stomach. "His foot."

Our son's foot presses into my palm through her stomach. "Wow, he's getting so strong."

"And big. I'm terrified to know what his birth weight is going to be. Why did I have to fall in love with a man with such a tall family?"

"To be fair, I'm the shortest one."

June rolls her eyes. "Six one is not short."

I could stand here and banter with her all day long. But we have somewhere to be. People waiting for us. I hold out my arm to her. "Would you come inside with me?"

"Of course. What's with the formality?"

I don't reply. June raises an eyebrow but doesn't ask another question. She wraps her hand around my bicep, and I lead her into the front hall.

Immediately, she notices how silent the house is. "Is this some weird surprise party? Are you throwing me a surprise baby shower?! Oh!" She claps her hands together. "I knew something was weird. Come out everyone! I figured it out."

I laugh and put my hands on her shoulders, softly massaging my thumbs into her back. "No, honey. But good guess."

June crosses her arms and looks up at me. "Do I have to guess or are you going to tell me?"

"Come on. Take my hand."

I lead her through the house and out into the backyard. The sun is starting to set, casting the sky above Lake Michigan in a pink and orange glow. Everything looks perfect: there are beautiful twinkling lights, a bounty of flowers courtesy of Rye's work, and, most importantly, all the people we love. Piper, my brothers, my Dad and Rye and baby Ivy, even Trevor and Rowan managed to put aside their differences to join us tonight.

"What's going..." June's eyes land on the most important guests of all. "Oh my God."

June's mother and father step out from the group. Her mother is practically her twin, but it's her father who shares her mismatched set of eyes. "Look at you, Junie. You're absolutely glowing."

June moves as fast as I've seen at seven months pregnant and leaps into their arms. "I can't believe you're here!" she squeals. They hold each other tightly. It brings a tear to everyone's eyes. Despite all of the hurt they've caused by being absent in her life, I know she loves them so deeply. They had to be here for this. Maybe their presence will begin a process of healing for her.

Piper is getting antsy, squirming in Keifer's arms. He's whispering to her something encouraging, but I can tell she's just as nervous as I am.

I have to do this now. For her.

I reach into my pocket and pull out the ring box I've had

for two months already and kneel down while June is still preoccupied with her parents.

"Oh my god! This is crazy! No wonder you've been acting so..." June turns around and her jaw goes slack at the sight of me. "...weird."

"Juniper Reed," I begin.

She puts her hand over her mouth. "Are you seriously doing this?" She glances over at everyone. "Is he serious?"

"Yes!" Piper announces and everyone laughs.

June smiles through the tears already streaming down her face. "This is crazy, this is..." Her eyes lock in mine. "You're crazy, Jarred."

"I haven't even done anything yet."

June flushes and takes a step toward me. "Sorry. Go ahead."

I start again. "Juniper Reed. When we met, we were just kids. You were my younger brother's weird best friend who only ate cucumbers if they were peeled."

"I still do that."

"I know you do. I peel them for you."

She grins.

"I never expected to fall in love with you. Or that you would ever have it in your heart to love me when we've known each other through all the awkward phases of our lives. Braces, acne..."

"Your buzzcut phase."

I laugh. "Yes, thanks for the reminder."

All eyes are on us. And yet, I feel like June and I are the only two people in the world.

"You're the most amazing woman I've ever met. You've got the kindest soul, the brightest smile..." I glance over at Piper and bite back tears. "You treat my daughter as if she was your own. I never thought I'd find someone I'd trust to care for her and love her the way I do. And it turned out she was at family dinner every Sunday night and I just never took the time to really see her."

June clasps her hands in front of her face and smiles bashfully.

"And on top of all of this, you're having my baby."

She touches the crest of her belly.

"We're already a family, June. Always have been, really. And I want nothing more than to make it official." I open the ring box and hold it up to her. "Will you marry me?"

June looks to Piper before answering. "What do you think, Piper?"

Piper blushes and nods.

June grins. "Then yes. Of course. More than of course, if that's possible."

Everyone claps and cheers as she holds out her hand to me. I slip the ring onto her finger: the row of three diamonds shines brilliantly. Our hands interlace together. I start to get up, but June surprises me and sinks down to the ground, throwing her arms around me and kissing me.

I feel nearly lighter than air. Nearly. There's still another question to be asked. I would argue it's more important than a proposal of marriage.

I break the kiss first and touch June's cheek. "I still have one more thing."

"Oh god. Is it the surprise baby shower *now*? Is this a joint proposal-baby shower? That's a new one."

I turn to Piper and give her the signal. She squirms out of Keifer's arms and rushes over to us, her yellow sundress shuffling loudly. In her hands, she clutches an envelope.

"What is this, Piper?" June asks.

Piper is acting shy. She looks at me.

"Go ahead, baby."

Piper holds out the envelope to June. June takes it slowly. "Should I open it?"

Piper nods vehemently.

"Okay..." June tears open the envelope and looks inside. Confusion passes over her face. "These are legal documents. For..."

"Would you be my real mommy?" Piper blurts out loudly. She smacks her hands against her mouth, almost shocked it came out.

June's eyes widen as she looks from Piper to the documents and then to me. She has so many questions.

"I had my lawyers get in touch with Meredith. They made an arrangement with her so that she would give up her parental rights." I don't even want to think about the alimony payments I'll be having to make, but they're completely worth it for my girls' happiness.

June blinks. "These are adoption papers..."

"Yes."

"I can adopt Piper?" She turns to Piper, eyes growing wider. "I can adopt you! I can be your real mom!"

Piper laughs. "Yes."

June throws the documents to the side and pulls Piper into her arms tightly. She's shaking. "Yes. Of course. Of course, I'll be your mother. There's nothing I want more."

I hold my breath as I witness them together. You wouldn't know from looking at them that June wasn't Piper's mother from the beginning. That's the kind of love she has to give to the world. If I can be half as giving with my love as June, I think I'll have lived a full life.

"Then you're my mommy, Mommy!" Piper yelps for the whole world to hear. She puts her hands against June's cheeks. "Don't cry! Are you sad?"

"No, no, no. Happy. So happy."

Piper looks around. "You're all crying! Why are you all crying? This is happy!"

I wrap my arms around June and Piper. This is my whole family right here in my arms, the one I've created. June, Piper, our little boy yet to be named or born. I kiss both of them and dry their tears. June touches my face. "Thank you."

"Thank *you*."

Piper wriggles in our arms and puts her lips up against June's belly. "Did you hear that, little brother? We have the same mommy!"

We both laugh. "Okay, I have one more surprise," I say softly to June.

"Is it dinner? I really hope it's dinner because I'm starving."

"It is! How did you know?"

We all get to our feet. Our family encloses around us with congratulations and hugs and kisses. Together, we walk over to the terrace where a beautiful summery meal has been catered. No one is to lift a finger tonight. It's all about the love we have for each other.

The dinner goes on late into the evening, past all of our bedtimes. I want to hold onto this euphoria as long as possible.

Once the sky has gotten dark and the candles are nearly burned through, I glance around the table at my family. There's an abundance of love here. So much *risk* for love. Dad and Rye set quite an example for that. So did June's parents by flying out here and accepting all the craziness that was us coming together. Keifer too, who didn't have to accept the love that bloomed between me and June but did and took care of it so tenderly.

"Daddy?" Piper asks quietly from her spot on my lap.

"Yes, honey."

"Will June... will Mommy be my mommy tomorrow too?"

I look at June. She's entrenched in a conversation with Rowan, a humongous smile on her face. She took the biggest risk of us all to love Piper and me and be willing to have a child with me. I'll never stop being grateful to her.

"Tomorrow, Piper," I whisper and then kiss her head gently. "Tomorrow. And every single day after that."